"Your father was my worst enemy," he grated

"No, Nick, don't say that."

His brief laugh was full of irony. "Darling, even you can't deny it. Open your eyes."

"I think if I do, you might kill me."

"I might have once. But that's in the past. My miserable, blighted, unforgettable past."

"Don't let it hurt you, Nick," Dana whispered. "You're no longer—"

"A nobody?" For a second she allowed herself to look into his brilliant, hostile eyes. "Is that what you were going to say, Miss Merriman? You're right, I'm not. And if I'm a millionaire today I have you to thank for it, because all I wanted from life was to get enough money to destroy everything you have!"

Books by Margaret Way

HARLEQUIN ROMANCES

HARLEQUIN PRESENTS

These books may be available at your local bookseller.

For a free catalog listing all titles currently available,
send your name and address to:

Harlequin Reader Service
P.O. Box 52040, Phoenix, AZ 85072-2040
Canadian address: Stratford, Ontario N5A 6W2

House of Memories

Margaret Way

Harlequin Books

TORONTO • NEW YORK • LONDON
AMSTERDAM • PARIS • SYDNEY • HAMBURG
STOCKHOLM • ATHENS • TOKYO • MILAN

Original hardcover edition published in 1983
by Mills & Boon Limited

ISBN 0-373-02609-9

Harlequin Romance first edition March 1984

CHAPTER ONE

KEITH arrived on the Friday evening just as Dana was thinking of closing up shop.

'Here's your boy-friend, Miss Merriman,' Jenny, her young assistant, called airily.

'*Friend*, dear.' Dana winced and looked up from her casual perusal of the latest French wallpapers.

Through the elegant glass and timber-framed façade of her small interior design shop, she could see Keith stepping out of his car on the other side of the street. Typically he locked it as though it might be stolen from right beneath their very eyes. Late afternoon spring sunshine gilded his blond hair and his tanned skin, caught the golden gleam of his very expensive watch. He looked as sleek and up-market as his metallic grey B.M.W.

'You've been seeing rather a lot of him lately,' Jenny observed darkly.

She could of course put her in her place, but Dana didn't have the heart to. Jenny was only seventeen years old, with a seventeen-year-old's penchant for a barrage of chatter. Dana, kinder than most, was inclined to be indulgent.

'That's the difference between you and him,' Jenny was now saying sagely. 'He wants to be your boy-friend and you only want him for a friend.'

Right on! 'Oh well, Jenny, that's my business to figure out,' Dana returned mildly.

'Mm, and you will!' Jenny agreed with enthusiasm, her over the shoulder smile as wholesome as cornflakes. 'I don't think Mr Vaughn likes me very much.' Jenny wasn't clever, but she was uncannily shrewd.

'Of course he does,' Dana lied. 'Who could *not* like you, Jenny?'

'Well ...' Jenny hesitated to think, couldn't, and beamed. 'Sad the way you've never got married,' she added kindly. 'You're so beautiful and everything.'

'Thanks, dear.' Dana had to grope at the desk to stand up.

'Gran says you could have had anyone you wanted, but your dad thought there wasn't anyone half good enough for you.'

'You know what they say, Jenny. Is *any* man worth the love of a good woman?'

'It's not as if you even look twenty-six,' Jenny reasoned, her large blue eyes travelling over Dana's slender, poised figure. 'With your hair out you'd look the same age as me.'

'I'm older, Jenny dear. Much, much older.'

'I expect it's because you always speak so proper. My boy-friend thinks you look a million bucks.'

'What, Dougie?' Dana was slightly taken aback, then her beautiful, rare smile rippled across her face.

'Yes, Dougie!' Jenny made a plaintive sound. 'I had to listen to him one evening telling me you're a flamin' work of art.'

'Oh, Jenny!' Weary as she was, Jenny always made her laugh. 'He's right, of course.'

'Of course!' Jenny gave a trilling little giggle. 'Shall I pop along, then? Mr Vaughn is almost here. Why do you suppose he always locks his car? Anyone would think a bank robber might jump in!'

Dana laughed and nodded. 'Some people think it pays to be prudent.' She turned back to her desk and opened a drawer. 'Here, I've put a little extra in your pay packet this week. You deserve it.' If only for making me laugh.

'I do?' Jenny sounded doubtful. 'You pay me enough now.'

'No, really—go on, please, take it.'

'Gee, thanks!' Jenny's pert little face was happy and touched. 'I might be able to get that dress now.'

'Yes, get it. We're supposed to be happy when we're young.'

'You would have to be the best boss in the world,' Jenny said fervently. 'Sandra—you know Sandra—told me before I started she could never work for a woman. They're bitchy and bossy— that sort of thing. She wouldn't know. Anyway, she hasn't even got a job.'

'Tell her to try Fordhams,' said Dana. 'They need a junior.'

'I'll tell her.' Jenny thrust her pay packet into her bag. 'I really enjoy working for you, Miss Merriman—but then you're a Merriman to start with. A real lady. Gran remembers when you used to have servants! It must have been marvellous being a Merriman.'

Ah, yes, a Merriman. Never a lesser mortal. The last surviving member of a once proud old family. A family that had long dominated this rich sheep and wheat region. And no prospect whatever of the name being carried on.

'What's the matter?' Jenny queried. 'You look sad. I haven't said anything to upset you, have I?'

'Heavens, no, Jenny.' Dana cut the girl short. 'I'm tired, that's all. Go off, now, and have a lovely weekend.'

'You too, Miss Merriman.'

They walked together to the gold-lettered front door and Dana said pleasantly: 'Say hello to your grandmother for me.'

'I always do,' Jenny assured her. 'Gran is always talking about the old days—about you and your family. Wasn't your twenty-first birthday party the biggest celebration this district has ever seen?'

'It's true it lasted for about a week.'

'And you were really engaged to Nick McMasters?'

'There's no escape in this town! I was, Jenny. For about three days.'

'Goodness, how awful!' Apparently Jenny's grandmother had failed to tell her that. 'It must have been funny, him coming from the flats and you coming from the big house on the hill. 'Course, it's all different now. He's the millionaire and you ... oh, I beg your pardon. You know what I mean.'

'Yes, Jenny.'

'He was on television the other night.'

'I must have missed it.' God, how deliberately!

'What a pity!' Jenny allowed her eyes to roll expressively. 'He's so *rugged*. Sorta like Burt Reynolds with a bit of that old 007—you know, Sean Connery, thrown in.'

Keith must have forgotten something, for he returned to his car. 'Yes, I suppose that type,' Dana agreed, as Jenny seemed to be hanging on her answer. 'Dark hair. Very dark eyes.'

'He's got Burt Reynolds' mouth and teeth, and

I just love dark moustaches! Gran said he was always a wild one, but brilliant. The guy on the T.V. called him a computer genius. Fancy owning all those companies—and he's only thirty-two! I could hardly understand a word he was saying, but he sounded so *good*—like the way people speak French. You can't understand it, but you like it. Ah well, you'd expect that from a Master of Science. They're different to the rest of us, aren't they?'

'Little doubt about that, Jenny.'

'Life's funny, isn't it?' Jenny concluded. 'Anyway, he looked much too bold a guy for you.'

'Why do you keep that kid?' Keith asked Dana when they were finally alone.

'I like her.' Also, she's a very acute observer.

'But surely you could have found someone more intelligent. More decorative than Jenny. After all, this is a flourishing decorator's business.'

'She's worth her weight in gold,' Dana assured him.

'And she's got an old granny to support.'

'Yes.' Dana put a hand to her nape and tilted back her head, momentarily shutting her eyes. 'Jenny's parents were killed in a road accident when she was three. She was thrown clear and survived. Life hasn't been easy for her, or her grandmother.'

'So you offered her a job?'

'Jobs are hard to come by, Keith.'

'Especially for someone like Jenny. She's the type of kid who's always spilling the beans. I could just imagine having her in my office.' Keith was a senior partner in the town's leading law firm.

Dana, following his line of thought, had to smile. Discretion wasn't one of Jenny's assets. She was alarmingly open and honest and it had to be admitted tactless without meaning the least harm. She would learn. Life was a great teacher, batterer of the open and honest.

'So what's your news?' Dana pretended an interest she didn't feel.

'Are you sure you're ready for it?'

'It's not bad, I hope?' Dana looked into Keith's bland, good-looking face.

'No, but I know it means a lot to you.' Keith stared directly and intently into her eyes. Her eyes were her most beautiful feature, very large and soft and the rarest of all colours—violet. She radiated what Keith thought of as style yet she was strangely provocative—a sensuality made up of delicacy and grace, of a lovely speaking voice and bred-in-the-bone good manners. True, she dressed rather severely and her thick, raven dark hair, in stunning contrast to her white skin, was drawn back austerely and coiled on her nape. But severity seemed to suit her. It drew attention to the purity of her bone structure, the slender perfection of her body. Keith wanted her and he meant to get her.

'Well?' Her lips were parted softly and a faint expression of alarm glimmered in her eyes.

'Don't look like that, darling.' He broke out of his reverie. 'I'm sorry if I went off somewhat. I was only thinking how beautiful you are, how cool yet curiously alluring.'

'Alluring?' Dana leaned back and smiled wryly.

'Yes. For some reason you always remind me of a gazelle—all big almond eyes, very delicate and wary.'

'Weary, more like it.' She shrugged and smiled. 'This has been a very hectic week.'

'Surely you prefer it to things being slow?'

'Of course. But it does have an effect on the way one feels.'

'You've got a very bright future in this kind of business,' Keith told her in a faintly patronising fashion. 'You've turned your exquisite taste to advantage, and it's such a nice thing for a woman to do.'

'*Proper* thing?'

'It's womanly and creative,' he insisted.

'And just about the only thing I *could* do.'

'Nonsense, darling. You're a clever girl.'

Dana's huge violet eyes went dreamy. 'Sometimes I think I'd rather be any one of my friends. They have husbands, children to adore. Properties to work that are actually labours of love.'

Keith reached over to refill his glass. 'I've always thought you never liked the idea of marriage?' he challenged her, his sharp eyes hooded.

How could she ever tell him she had been blighted by first love; a passion so intense it was even now indestructible. 'Actually I would love to get married,' she parried lightly. 'To the man I love.'

'Ah!' Keith tossed off his drink. 'You don't love anyone yet, I take it?'

'I enjoy your company very much, Keith. You know that.' She smiled at him, but her lovely eyes were sad.

'I know.' His firm mouth thinned. 'I know how you feel. But I'm going to change it, you'll see. I'm going to pursue you until you're so weak you'll fall into my arms!'

'We'll see.' She laughed and the remoteness faded from her face.

'Come to dinner with me tonight,' Keith pleaded with a feeling of frustration he disliked.

'But we're having dinner tomorrow night.'

'Does that matter? Neither of us wants to eat alone.'

'O.K.,' she said. 'But only if you're going to tell me your news.'

'No big deal.' Despite his words Keith was watching her very closely. 'Merrilands is changing hands again.'

'Oh?' Dana absorbed it in absolute stillness.

'Yes.' Keith kept his eyes on her. 'Stafford has finally thrown in the towel.'

'Well, he was only playing at being a grazier.'

'So he was.' Keith glanced away from her cool face to his immaculately manicured hands. 'He had the money to buy Merrilands and he did. Just another status symbol. I'm told it all started when Ingram left him.'

'I knew Bert wouldn't stick it. I just hope he has enough for his retirement.' Bert Ingram had given more than forty years of his life to Merrilands. He had worshipped her father. He had seen her father destroyed.

'I expect so. He's a canny old bird.'

'So who bought it?' Dana asked, realising Keith was playing some long-drawn-out little game of his own.

'Some company,' he said mildly. 'We didn't act for Stafford, but we hear most of what's going on. It changed hands at a few million over the reserve. Apparently the crowd that bought it wanted it pretty badly.'

'It's a magnificent property,' said Dana. Her

hands were trembling so she hid them beneath the top of her desk.

'I figure the new owner, manager, whatever, might send for you to restore the old place to its former glory. The Staffords might have money, but they have the most appalling taste. You've no idea!'

'I'm glad I didn't see it.'

'No, you never would go to any of their functions.'

'I didn't have the heart.'

'Thea Stafford took quite a different view. She always held it against you, you know.'

'I'm sorry.'

'The only person I ever heard call Miss Dana Merriman a stuck-up snob.'

'I don't think I've ever been that.' Suddenly restless, Dana stood up. 'Anyway, I've been called worse names.'

'Not in this town!' Keith's smooth, good-looking face looked shocked. 'You're one of the few people everyone manages to like—even the women.'

'I suspect it's because I never make them feel threatened,' Dana smiled.

'That could be significant,' Keith agreed. 'For all your allure, you act like a sister to their husbands. It's really quite extraordinary. Something about you keeps a distance between you and the men who admire you—some chasm, some terrible sadness. There, I've said it.' He came forward and took Dana by the elbows. 'Can't I make you long for a husband of your own?'

'Keith,' her expression softened magically, 'I like you, very much—but don't rush me.'

'That's because you're not in love. If you were in love you'd want to be rushed off your feet.'

'I suppose so.' Now her expression went bleak.

'What are you thinking about?' He tilted up her head so he could stare into her eyes.

'I'm thinking we're very much on view, Keith.'

'There it is again—evasion!'

'I'm not being mean to you,' she persisted. 'Old Mrs Edmonds is sitting on the bench across the street watching in here like a movie screen.'

'Let her.' Nevertheless Keith released her and swung round. 'Oh, charming, she's spying on us!'

'Never.' Dana smiled. 'At over eighty she feels entitled to know exactly what's going on in this town.'

'If you won't marry me,' said Keith just a little angrily, 'can't we at least live in sin?'

'I don't think that would be good for the firm. Or the people you deal with.'

'Don't be flippant, darling. I'm serious.'

And I can never be serious, Dana knew.

CHAPTER TWO

THE telephone broke into the quietness of the house.

'Dana?' It was a bright voice, full of warmth and enthusiasm.

'Oh, hi, Vicki. I meant to ring you today, but got tied up.'

'That's all right, love.' Vicki was Dana's closest woman friend. 'Listen, I suppose you've heard about Merrilands?'

'Yes.' Dana unclipped her ear-ring and set it down. 'Keith told me this afternoon.'

'About time that pain in the neck Stafford pulled out.'

'Bert left as well,' Dana pointed out.

'Yes, I know. Some company bought it, some crowd Dave has never heard of. Do you want him to find out?'

'No, Vicki. I can't let it mean anything to me any more.'

'Want to come over for lunch tomorrow? It's Saturday, remember?'

'That will be lovely.'

'Great! Now, I have to go,' said Vicki. 'Tim is rapidly on the move these days. I used to worry and worry if he'd ever get up and walk, now I never get a breather. How about staying on for dinner?'

'Keith has already arranged something,' Dana told her.

'Seeing a lot of him aren't, you?' Older and

wiser than Jenny, Vicki kept all trace of
disapproval out of her tone, but Dana knew
neither Vicki nor Dave had ever really taken to
Keith.

'We can't all get a gorgeous husband,' she
smiled.

Vicki laughed, then sobered. 'Did you see Nick
on TV the other night?'

'No.'

'Come on, love, you can talk to me.'

'I didn't see him, Vick. I couldn't have borne
to.'

'Dear God!' Vicki fetched up a sad, heartfelt
sigh. 'And you were the last one I ever thought
would play with fire.'

'Well, I did.'

'But *years* have passed, love. Listen, I have to
go.' Vicki gave a muffled shriek. There was a
smashing sound in the background. Vicki yelled:
'See you!' and hung up.

Keith arrived promptly about thirty minutes
later.

'New dress?' he asked.

'Do you like it?'

'Need you ask? You always look supremely
elegant.' He bent his head and kissed her cheek
and she caught a wave of expensive and spicy
male lotion. Suddenly she didn't want to go out
with him, to be with him at all. Rejection
overwhelmed her, and she felt terrified she would
be like that all her life. If there was any hope at
all for her, she had to escape the past.

'Hmm, lovely. Shall we go?' Kissing her cheek,
Keith had not seen her eyes.

The head waiter at April's greeted them like

Royalty, escorting them to their usual table that looked out over sloping lawns and gardens to a man-made lake afloat with waterlilies and swans.

'Lovely place, isn't it?' said Keith by way of a change. He usually said: 'I love this place, don't you?'

Dana loved the view, but she often thought the décor was a little extreme. The restaurant had been better run by the last owners, an Italian couple, but the new owner, April Radcliffe, had completely changed the concept. Dana could see her on the other side of the room, moving through the tables like some spectacular flamingo.

'Ah, there's April!' said Keith with satisfaction. 'Amazing woman, isn't she? I knew when she first came to us she was just what this town wanted.'

Eventually April found her way to their table.

'Keith, Dana! Lovely to see you.' April smiled brilliantly at Dana while her hand lingered on Keith's shoulder.

'I was just saying to Dana how much we love this place!' Keith exclaimed.

'I'm so glad.' April leaned down closer to him. 'And so very generous for Dana to say. I didn't realise she was so good, otherwise I would never have used another decorator.'

'I don't think even Dana could have done better,' Keith smiled. 'But really, the place is *you*.'

April acknowledged the intended compliment with a little graceful shrug. She was a tall, glamorous blonde by choice, physically well endowed with round, voluptuous breasts, a comparatively tiny waist and curving hips. A

Rubens, Dana always thought, with those funny little sinful smirks. Temptation.

'What a truly handsome woman she is!' Keith commented later, when April had finally given up pressing her bosom inadvertently against his shoulder.

'She likes you as well.'

'Really?' Keith looked enormously pleased.

'How little you men know!'

Keith's fine skin blushed. 'Anyway, she's come a long way since she first came to me for advice. It always amazes me how strong women really are. I mean, you might have been reared in the lap of luxury, but April wasn't. She only married a rich man and he didn't look after her at all well. Willed most of the money to his first family. Upsetting for April.'

'He *did* leave her enough to buy the Blackman place and this restaurant,' Dana pointed out.

'Maybe.' Keith detected Dana's faint lack of sympathy. 'But we can't overlook her ambition and drive. You're a low key personality compared to April, but you have every bit as much courage.'

'Thank you, Keith,' Dana said with an air of meekness.

'Yes, darling, very courageous indeed.' Either Keith hadn't assimilated the mockery or chose to ignore it. He dropped his eyes back to the menu, propping it up against the table. 'What say we take April's advice and start with the *délice d'avocat*?'

They were together for three more hours, for most of which Keith did the talking. 'You're unusually tense tonight,' he told her as Dana hunted up the front door keys. 'I expect it's the news about Merrilands that's upset you.'

'I've long reconciled myself to losing Merrilands, Keith.' She longed to say goodnight, but it was just too rude.

'How could one ever reconcile oneself to losing a magnificent property like that?' he challenged her. 'I know how you feel, Dana. Won't you let it out?'

Inside the hallway he took her determinedly into his arms. 'Trust me, darling. Let me help you. Whatever it is you've locked up inside I'm here to help.'

'But I don't think I need help, Keith,' Dana said gently. 'I'm trying my best to make something of my life and I hope I'm succeeding.'

'Succeeding!' Keith threw back his head meaningfully, 'Darling, you're a beautiful woman, and you're alone.'

'Do you think a woman so weak and needy she can't function without a man?'

'That's every man's basic assumption.' He smiled at her with playful good humour. 'A woman can't be fulfilled without forming an intimate relationship with a man.'

'At some part of her life, I agree. The really lucky ones maintain and live with that bond, but there are plenty of us left who have to shape our lives alone. That's the way it has to be for any number of men and women. It isn't exactly easy to fall deeply in love, and a lost love can leave plenty of scars.'

'Come here and sit down.' With his arm around her Keith guided her into the living room, decorated in a style as distinct and elegant as Dana herself. 'For the first time you've said something that's close to the truth.'

'Oh?' Dana sank into the sofa and pulled away from him quietly.

'How am I to help you, Dana?' he said, and took hold of her hand. 'I love you, but you isolate yourself from love.'

'I don't, Keith, believe me. It's my dearest wish to love someone, but I can't *make* it happen.'

'You won't let it happen,' he said bluntly.

'Have you every been in love with anyone else but me, Keith?' she challenged him.

'Darling, I'm thirty-four!'

'So that at least once you were very, very serious. What happened?'

'I wasn't really ready for marriage, Dana,' he told her. 'Emotional attachments tend to interfere with the business of forging a career.'

'You couldn't have been in love, Keith,' she murmured.

'Certainly not what I feel for you. In the early years it's more important for a man to get ahead. First things first, Keith, my mother used to say to me. It was absolutely impossible to marry my first love. She was a sweet thing then, but she wouldn't suit me now. Men change.'

'Don't they ever!'

'And you're still grieving for McMasters, aren't you?'

For an instant Dana was paralysed. Keith had never ever referred directly to the past.

'Don't be angry with me,' Keith said gently, stroking her cheek. 'It has to come out in the open some time. I heard about you and Nick McMasters the same day I came here. There's always someone around waiting to tell you everything, and of course McMasters is something of a celebrity—the local boy made better than good. What happened to you two?'

'Surely you were told?' Dana was long used to hiding her distress.

'I can understand it,' said Keith. 'Any father of an adored only daughter demands the best for her. McMasters must have been pretty awful in those days.'

'Awfully poor.' Dana's lovely face came alive with anger. 'His father was killed when his crop-duster packed up in mid-air. His mother nearly died afterwards of shock. The baby she was carrying *did* die. Afterwards she had to do domestic work to support herself and Keith, but he soon found lots of jobs around the district to help her. I never knew him when he didn't act like a man, and I first met him when I was six years old. He was twelve and my father was very taken with him—*then*.'

'Keep talking, Dana,' Keith said.

'There's little to be said. Everyone knew I adored Nick when I was a child. He knew everything I ever wanted to know. He was so vivid and interesting and kind. No young boy could have been kinder to an annoying little girl.'

'Surely he *had* to be, as you were Grant Merriman's daughter?' Keith murmured dryly.

'Nick didn't give a damn about anyone. Only his mother. My father used to laugh and say he turned the tables on everyone. He was always brilliant, always someone. He never felt shame because they had no money. He hated the fact that his delicate little mother had to do physical work.'

'She worked at the house didn't she?'

Dana nodded. 'She did some washing and ironing, took mending home. She was a wonderful needlewoman. I know she used to make dresses for the little girls on the flats.'

'They weren't good enough for the right side of town?'

'Certainly they were good enough, but few people were good enough to ask her. She made me a dress once and I loved it. I can remember it to this day, but Mrs Cameron, our housekeeper, gave it away to a charity. Such cheap material couldn't be allowed to touch my patrician skin. I remember I was having a glass of milk in the kitchen when Nick came to call. He was never allowed in the front, only the back. He'd seen *my* dress, the dress his mother had lavished such care on, on one of the little girls in the neighbourhood and he wanted to know why. Mrs Cameron told him. She never even tried to be tactful, and Nick went for her suddenly in a way that made her afraid.'

'You mean he attacked her?' Keith asked incredulously. 'I heard he was wild.'

'Nick never had to physically attack anyone. He could annihilate them with words. At the time he was only a fourteen-year-old boy with no shoes on, but he made Mrs Cameron accept him as a man. Mrs Cameron just fell apart. She even made an apology of sorts, but ever afterwards she always called him an arrogant, headstrong boy, a boy that was certain to get into trouble. I think it was Mrs Cameron who first started the rumours about how wild he was.'

'He must have been a bit wild?' Keith demurred.

'He was very high-mettled. He went out of his way to antagonise a lot of people, important people who liked to remind him he came from the river flats. On the other hand, for someone so quick and clever he could be amazingly patient. There wasn't a piece of machinery he didn't seem to know about or what was wrong with it when it broke down. Grown men used to ask his advice and even say thank you when he told them. They were the workers, of course. None of our gentlemen farmers would have thanked him. Not even my father. He would have said: 'Good, Nick!' and perhaps smiled. For years my father was very entertained by Nick. He foretold that Nick would either make a wonderful name for himself or commit murder.'

'*Murder?*' Keith echoed.

'An exaggeration, of course. But I think Nick would have killed anyone who ever hurt his mother. Or me. For years I was the little sister he'd always wanted. The one who had died.'

'And afterwards it was different. He fell in love with you?'

'He dared to love me, yes.'

'But what did he expect!' Keith sounded as amazed as once Grant Merriman had been. 'He ought to have known your father would want great things for you. No barefoot boy.'

'When Nick asked me to marry him he already had a brilliant degree,' said Dana. 'His mother died when he was in high school and he had some kind of nervous breakdown, but he achieved in six months what it took everyone else to do in two years, and did it ten times better. He had so many part-time jobs I don't know how he never collapsed from exhaustion, but he was always very strong.'

'He reminds me of a footballer,' Keith commented rather disparagingly. 'I mean, he looks nothing like what he's supposed to be.

More like some fast-talking, super-sharp con-man.'

'That's the black eyes and the black moustache. Men of science can be big powerful-looking men with broad shoulders.'

'I suppose so,' Keith frowned. 'I can't see you with him at all. You're so lovely, so refined. He really does look and act like some damned exhibitionist movie star. Didn't you see him on television the other night?'

'No.'

'Did you sleep with him, Dana?' Keith asked.

'Yes.'

'My God!' There was silence for a while. 'No wonder your father hated him!'

'My father didn't hate him, Keith,' Dana said gravely. 'My father feared him as a rival for the most important person in my life. After my mother died, Father and I drew very close together. We only had one another. My love for Nick in no way affected my love for my father, but my father couldn't see that. I don't think it was ever Nick's lack of money or social position that incurred my father's absolute opposition. My father was certain Nick was going to give an extraordinary account of himself in life. It's strange when you think about it. My father *did* say Nick would finish up a millionaire, that nothing and no one would stop him, because that was the way Nick was. My father, although I loved him, perhaps destroyed my life. The really significant thing was not that Nick came from the river flats or our friends would be scandalised. My father couldn't bear the idea of sharing me with Nick. Certainly he didn't really want me to get married, but he knew I had to. I'm sure it would have been quite all right if I'd become engaged to any one of six or seven of my father's friends' sons. My father was very possessive, but he hid it well. Many of the boys I knew would have accepted Father's exalted position in my life. I was Grant Merriman's daughter first and someone else's wife second. Nick was always psychoanalysing someone. Once he did it to my father, right to his face. I tried to stop him, but he didn't spare Father. I knew that night my father would never let me marry Nick. Nick knew him too well.'

'But surely even sheltered young girls dig in their heels. If you loved him so much why didn't you two just run off?' In spite of himself Keith was moved by the old story.

'Perhaps I might have, only Nick wouldn't run anywhere. He said we had to stay and face it, do it right. I just couldn't believe it when my father said we might get engaged.'

'Could it be he suspected you might run away?'

'He knew I was helpless between the two of them. Neither of them really considered me. I was only the prize. Three days after we became engaged my father suffered what I believed to be, then, a heart attack. He fixed it with his friend, our family doctor, to tell me the worst. Nick laughed when I told him and I was in a state of fear and total panic. I loved my father—I had reason to love him. He had devoted his whole life to me.'

'So he wanted to tie you to his side and to do that he had to develop a heart condition?'

'I believed him in my love and loyalty. I fought bitterly with Nick. Even Nick was surprised. I've always been too non-aggressive for my own good, so when Nick turned on the mockery I went over completely to my father's side.'

'Just like that. All at once?'

'I gave Nick back his ring. I threw it at him and he never even bothered to pick it up. The ring cost him every penny he had. Weeks and months and years of hard work. Nick knew he loved me long before I came to see him as my lover. Even when I threw his ring at him I was convinced nothing could ever come between us. I was simply someone slow to anger who suddenly blew up. Nick and my father were both overpowering personalities and I thought then they were both trying to stone me out. Which to this day I believe they were. I was just the fair maiden, the beautiful idiot they were duelling over. I wasn't a real person. Neither of them really cared about me, just themselves. It was war and the spoils went to the stronger. My father collapsed one night after I tried to talk to him, and I knew then I couldn't leave him.'

'Poor little Dana!' Keith said softly.

'When I told Nick he went into a rage. Unlike me, Nick had a volcanic temper. For the first time ever when he made love to me he hurt me. He wanted to hurt me—he even said he did. I thought he was possessed, and I'd never live through it. Anyway, I didn't care. Nick's brutality was better than anyone else's love.'

'Hell!' Keith's exclamation sounded bitter and strained. 'As you say, if he'd really loved you he could never have treated you that way.'

'When I opened my eyes some time in the dawn he covered me with kisses, looking down at me and begging forgiveness. "You always knew I wasn't a gentleman, Dana," ' he said.

'Brute,' Keith muttered. 'One would know that just looking at him. Your father in practising a little deceit was only trying to save you.'

'If that was his intention.' There was an ironic edge on Dana's voice now. 'You know my father and one of his closest friends were killed in a light aircraft crash?'

'Yes, shortly before I came here. Pilot error, wasn't it?'

'Yes, that came out at the inquiry. All three of them were killed. After the funeral Arthur, that's our doctor, told me the truth.'

'Why? It was so pointless.'

'My father persuaded Arthur against his own principles. Arthur is very fond of me. Unexpectedly he was one of Father's few friends to champion Nick. He thought I should be told. I'd worried myself sick about Father's health, but there'd never been anything remotely wrong with his heart.'

'The thing was he was acting in your best interests,' Keith maintained. 'I think it quite disgusting that McMasters should have made love to an innocent young girl.'

'Then let me astound you, Keith, and say I never stopped provoking Nick until he lost control. I was crazy, mad with love for him. It was unbearable *not* to be made love to.'

'My God!' Keith turned to stare at her. 'And you won't even let me caress your breasts! I thought you were a puritan, but you're really a phoney.'

'I suppose.' Dana drew a deep jagged breath. 'Or maybe I'm condemned to be faithful to a memory all my life.'

'What rot!' Keith shook his head. He looked at

her with some vague shift in his manner. 'You know, the trouble with you, Dana, you're trading on one bad experience. You're playing out some tormented bit of theatre. I know what a great reader you are. You're dramatising your own situation. I thought all along you were strangely provocative for an ice maiden. Now you tell me you had some powerful sex relationship going when you were still a young girl. The things one learns!'

'Surely you didn't have the idea that I'd never known love?'

'Your affair with McMasters is pretty well documented.'

'And incidentally, Keith, *my* business.'

'Which is fine if I didn't love you.' Keith shook his fair head. 'Haven't you ever thought another affair might cure your obsession?'

'Certainly.' Dana looked at him and arched one of her delicate, winged eyebrows. 'I stayed home a lot, but I did have lots of admirers. For my own sake and for the sake of the property. In those days no one, even I, knew how heavily Father was into speculative deals. The first intimation was when BASCO folded. My father lost two million. Even then we carried on. When other men sat on their acquired holdings my father inexplicably decided to lash out. He knew everything there was to know about being a gentleman farmer, but very little about big business and the real con-men. I *felt* some of the people Father had to the house weren't to be trusted, but Father was drinking more by this time and rather keen on taking gambles. He'd always been a rich man. He never thought he could be anything else. He always piloted his own plane, but because he was depressed and worried he let one of his so-called friends do the flying. The rest you know. I had to sell Merrilands and by the time our affairs were settled I was no longer a highly eligible heiress. I was a working girl rather better off than most. I was able to buy this house and start a business and still have some left over. I was lucky.'

'And McMasters never tried to contact you?'

'He drove through the night to be with me. I refused to see him. In fact, I had him moved on by the police. One of them tried to strong-arm him and he sent them both flying. He spent the night in jail, but they remembered him from earlier times and didn't press charges. In fact there didn't seem to be any hard feelings on either side. Nick had that effect on his own sex. Hero material. Why shouldn't a guy fight for his girl?'

'They'd certainly press charges with *me*!' Keith experienced anger and resentment. 'So he went away?'

'He wrote to me from the jail, and one of the constables even brought the letter up. He was on Nick's side. I didn't even read it but tore it up in front of him. I never heard from Nick again.'

'And you've been lucky, in my opinion. I'm not surprised your father thought he'd finish with a criminal record.'

'Well, he hasn't, has he?' snapped Dana.

'Don't get angry,' Keith pleaded.

'I'm not angry, Keith.' I'm dying of pain and loneliness.

'Well, look at me, then.'

Dana did so and he leaned forward with a yearning not unmixed with a rather venomous male resentment. For months now she had been holding him off at a virginal arm's length, so it was intolerable to hear about her erotic adventure with a man who even on TV came over as a man who was positively, destructively sexual. Dana must have been easy prey for a villain like that.

'*Keith!*' Dana protested when she was able.

'It's perfectly simple,' he said harshly, 'you can't really continue to expect me to treat you like a debutante when on your own admission you've already abandoned yourself to love.'

'Oh yes, indeed I *can*!' she returned, unperturbed. 'It's extraordinary how men see themselves with all the rights. Underneath that expensive suit you're really a chauvinist wolf in sheep's clothing, Keith. Because I was once passionately in love and surrendered up what you men put such store by, I can never expect to be treated with dignity again. I don't know why on earth I told you. You only thought you wanted to know.'

'I did want to know, Dana,' Keith answered rigidly. 'By the same token, you must accept that if we're going to continue to see one another I'm entitled to more than a few chaste kisses.'

'Exactly *why*?' Dana faced him and for the first time Keith saw her violet eyes blazing.

'Now, now, don't get angry.' He took a deep breath. 'All I mean is I'm in love with you and you're treating me like a platonic friend.'

'I should allow you into my bed?'

'I wish you would.' He groaned aloud. 'You frighten me, Dana. You're a beautiful, highly desirable . . .'

'Sex object?'

'*Woman*, I was going to say, yet you've got

yourself locked into some priggish, celibate lifestyle.'

'Perfect for a woman when she's not in love.'

'You're cruel.' Keith's golden skin lost colour.

'I'm sorry.' Dana went to move, but he stopped her. 'I don't mean to hurt you, Keith, but you can't expect more than I'm prepared to give. If you want, we won't see each other for a time. Very likely I'm not good for you.'

'Darling!' He kissed her twice on her delicately scented neck. She always seemed to wear the same fragrance, a scent he associated with her alone. Gardenia, rose? He didn't know. It was so beautiful yet elusive. It was Dana. 'There.' He turned her face and kissed her gently on the mouth. 'You ask the impossible, you know that?'

'I don't want to make you unhappy.' She didn't. Neither did she want to invite him into her bedroom.

'Have you ever thought your experience with McMasters might have revolted you? Turned you off a normal relationship with another man?'

This time she did stand up, taking refuge by the big bay window, staring out into the darkened garden. 'Yes, I have thought of it, Keith, but I don't really want to talk about it. It was agonising enough at the time.'

'Why is it,' Keith said sharply, 'that good women always fall for bad men?'

'I don't know any bad men,' Dana attempted a smile to lighten the atmosphere.

'You knew a ferociously ambitious young upstart who ravished you.'

'Vanity, Keith. Vanity. You'd ravish me as well.'

'At least I haven't so far. I expect McMasters didn't even ask?'

'Sometimes, Keith, you don't have to ask. You know that. Anyway, that's all in the past. One of these days I'll recover.'

'Not as long as you cling to it,' Keith told her, his light eyes sharpening over her. 'What you've done, my girl, is build a stockade around your heart. And I'll tell you another thing—you're keeping McMaster's image alive. I'll bet you've even got a photograph of him around someplace?'

'If I have I'd have to search for it very hard.'

'You've got it,' said Keith. He glanced down at his watch and stood up. 'Why can't you be honest about it?'

'If you want to see Nick's picture, Keith, I expect I could find it.' Dana's face was lit with that same astonishing anger and some mockery.

'Wouldn't it be better to just tear it up?' He walked to her and put his faintly trembling hands on her shoulders. 'You want children, don't you, Dana? A family? McMasters will never come back to you. You sent him away. I wouldn't care to humiliate a man like that. Behind the snapping black eyes and the white smile I thought I spotted a tiger. Surely there could never have been any point in trying to tame a dangerous animal?'

'You realise a lot of women do it, of course?'

'I know you really hate men, Dana,' Keith accused her stiffly. 'It's never really occurred to me until now.'

'Fantastic! You may have hit on it.' She smiled at him wryly.

'Bitch. Witch.' He looped his arm around her waist and drew her to him. 'You make me mad with wanting you.'

Dear God, if only she could feel the same! She

wasn't proud of her resistance, of quelling Keith's trembling desire. But love could not be forced. The more urgently one desired it, the more it shrank away. She knew he was furiously frustrated and instinctively, woman-like, her body yielded, but she knew it wouldn't help either of them to be urged into bed. She didn't love Keith, and she had only once in her desperate misery slept with a man she didn't love and it had been a disaster. She had no heart or mind for sexual adventures. Better nothing than a miracle reduced to something meaningless.

She slipped instantly out of Keith's arms while he looked after her helplessly. He was crowding her, he knew, forcing the pace—but damn it all, she wasn't a vulnerable young girl. Well, she looked vulnerable, full of heartbreak, but she was twenty-six years old. She couldn't stay forever suspended in the past.

'Keith,' she said gently, '*why* do you want me?'

'Hell!'

She felt rather than saw him shake his head. 'I know I hurt you, disappoint you, and I don't want to. I'm beginning to feel I could never really be what you want. You deserve a whole woman, and I'm wasting your time.'

'No, don't say that.' He knew he was being very foolish rushing her. 'You're the most wonderful thing to come into my life. You know we're very happy together. We get on so well. It's just this physical thing—all the emotions you have dammed up inside. One way or another the men in your life have really hurt you. Your father, although he loved you, wasn't strictly fair to you, and the less said about McMasters the better. Rather than grieve for him I think you should go down on your knees and thank God you escaped him. How could you, a gentle woman, live in that man's shadow? I detest those bold, exuberant types. They may handle lots of things—power with ease, but I wonder what it would be like to try and live with them. Peace, serenity, is very important. I don't think one could have that with a dynamo—moreover, a dynamo who comes across like an actor. It makes me unhappy to even think of you two together!'

'Please don't, Keith.' Dana's hand moved uncertainly to her right temple. 'You know nothing about Nick. He was kind, kind, *kind*.'

'And unlike you, darling, a challenge to every woman he meets. If you ever bothered to look in any of your glossy magazines you'd find he has a wonderful time. It's ridiculous when you come to think of it—here you are, remote and impregnable, mourning a lost love, and he's playing the devil with the best-looking women in the country.'

'You might do it yourself in his place.'

'Never.' Keith went to her and lifted her chin. 'I love you, Dana, and I'm a very determined man. Patient, too, when I have to be.'

'Understand, Keith—I can't promise anything!' Her violet eyes were huge and distressed. 'I don't want to spoil anything for you, waste your time. There are other attractive women you could be seeing. Think back to tonight. April Radcliffe would be delighted to help you pass the time.'

'April?' Keith lifted his head as though testing the air. 'Do you really think so?'

'You must have noticed?'

'Good lord!'

'I haven't the least objection if you want to take her to dinner some time.'

'What?' Keith looked affronted. 'You're impossible, Dana. You really are.'

'Maybe for you.' Suddenly Dana wanted to bring this thing to a head. 'I offered you friendship, Keith. Not to be your lover. I've never misled you. I can't just go to bed with a man, though everyone else seems to be rushing there. If it's not enough to enjoy one another's company then we must split up. I don't want to be pressured into a sexual relationship when I'm not ready for it. Sex isn't fun for me, it's more like the miracle of creation. I don't want to sound precious, but that's the way I am.'

'I know, darling.' Keith took her hand. 'Do you think I would want a woman who offered herself freely? But you must show a little enthusiasm. You could, if you'd only let yourself go. I exect it's because you've led a peculiar sort of life and now you're too much alone.'

She laughed then, a rising little laugh that had a touch of hysteria. How strangely Keith tried to console her!

'Dana?' Keith was looking down at her with anxious eyes.

'It's all right. I'm a little tired.'

'Yes, you must be.' Prudently Keith bent to kiss her and moved towards the door. Poor, poor girl! He felt an agony of possessive love. The sooner she realised *he* was the solution, her big hope in life, the sooner she could stop all her suffering. He actually felt hatred for that scoundrel Nick McMasters. He could literally smash him to pieces, big man or not.

Keith almost ran down the short flight of steps

and out to his car parked in the drive. The only thing to do, he thought while he unlocked it, was to take her by storm. Shock therapy was what she needed. It would be what the likes of McMasters would try. What man could ever rely on what a woman *said*? God knows they craved to be mastered. The only way to get out of an impossible situation was to end it, one way or the other. She might scream, but if he didn't get release soon, he might start screaming himself.

Inside her bedroom Dana started talking to herself. Are you a real woman or aren't you?

The young woman in the mirror said nothing.

She sat down at the dressing table, continuing to stare at herself. What really went on behind that delicate, rather gentle face? Those big, haunted eyes? Were they becoming vacant? She lifted her hand to the pins in her hair and pulled them out, and her hair ran in a silky black river down her back.

You look simple, she said, but you're really very complicated. Keith's aggrieved face rose in front of her and she moaned. Beyond the niceness he was really trying to browbeat her into bed. If she continued to see him, could she really postpone it indefinitely? Just imagine! At sixteen virginity was everything; at twenty-six it was a cause for alarm. She decided if she really loved Keith there would be no problem at all. She wasn't suffering from a severe repression, some manifestation of an acute neurosis arising from 'the peculiar sort of life' she had led. Keith had been quick to alight on that, but the truth was Dana couldn't overcome her own nature, the woman within; a woman who couldn't accommodate herself to having a string of lovers. Others did it without a thought. Some of them even had husbands. She stared sadly at herself, then stood up.

Where was that photo of Nick? *Where?* she asked herself with genuine anguish. If she didn't free herself of Nick she would have to kill herself.

Well after twelve o'clock she found what she was looking for. She jumped down from the chair and started back towards her bedroom carrying a dusty, leather-bound photo album.

She couldn't bear to look at it and that was the truth of it. Merrilands. Her beloved father whose treachery still wrenched her heart. Her pets. Her pony. Duchess, her beautiful mare. Crowds of her friends. They were all here in this book. Dana clutched the album to her with exactly the same feeling as Pandora with the forbidden box. She was so agitated the blood had drained right away from her white skin.

She opened the album up and a dozen small snapshots fell out. She saw her own radiant childhood face and for a few moments the agitation subsided. She had been such a happy little girl. 'Too sweet to spoil.' She didn't know exactly who had said that, but it was the general feeling she knew. She had grown up adored and adoring. There was her father with her on his shoulder. The tears started to her eyes.

Such a handsome man he had been, a man of charm and authority, and, it had to be admitted when anyone crossed him—arrogance. But finally that beloved man had betrayed her. It seemed a very long time ago, yet the pain was there, ready to reopen with the pages of an album.

No one they ever knew seemed to be left out. Alicia, tall and elegant. Alicia had connived at everything to marry her father and it all had failed. It was simply that Grant Merriman had lived overwhelmingly for his only child. He did have women friends, but none of his relationships had ever resulted in a second marriage. It might have been better for Dana if they had.

There were photos of her and Vicki before every party. How young they were, how pretty. In those days she had worn her hair differently in a dark, floating cloud. These days she was almost dragging the deep natural wave out. How Vicki had envied her her abundant curly hair.

It's not fair. You don't *need* curly hair. You're *beautiful!*

Now Vicki was happily married with a wonderful little boy. There was no doubt Vicki had the best of it. Vicki didn't believe in playing with fire. Inevitably it led to disaster.

And so: *Nick.*

Dana's heart quivered at the first sight. A pair of brilliant black eyes, a sweet curving mouth. Without even realising what she did, she lifted the large glossy press print and kissed it.

The kiss was not returned, would never be returned. God, what a fool she was! She gave a little jerky indrawn sob. So many memories violently returned. She and Nick lying together in the darkness. The passion neither of them could control. She felt herself go molten, then emotions spurted up that choked her.

When had it begun? Very soon after her sixth birthday. She had, until then, only loved and admired her father, then Nick arrived at Merrilands and sealed himself into her heart and mind. They belonged to very different back-grounds which had never mattered to her, or indeed to Nick. What had mattered, what her father in the beginning had approved of, was the genuine loving bond that sprang up between a small girl and a young boy.

While the McMasters boy was about, the Merrilands little heiress was well protected and happy. Any little dangers and Nick was there to turn them aside. He had loved and protected her, even helped her with her studies, exploding such notions that anything could be difficult. With his incessant curiosity and his hunger for knowledge and self-advancement, Nick had acquired a formidable bank of knowledge which he imparted or withheld according to how he was approached. Mrs Cameron, their housekeeper, had often spoken of him as possessing 'powers' much in the same way she would have spoken of the devil, and it was true Nick did have the uncanny ability to dominate other people. She had always thought it the power of a fine mind. A mind, as he had proved, far out of the ordinary. Nick was family. She was the little sister he had lost, in his heart.

That lasted for nearly ten years. Then the fire was set. The slow-burning realisation that their relationship had crossed over into another dimension. It had stupefied her until her eighteenth year, protected her in a way, and Nick never said anything, gave no sign. Only his eyes—brilliant, intense, thrilling. She had never seen another pair of eyes remotely like them.

Of course Nick had come a long way. He was already a Bachelor of Science, studying for his Master's. Scholarships and countless part-time jobs had helped him in his climb, and a small legacy from old Colonel Parker. The Colonel had always taken a keen interest in Nick's brilliant progress. He had been a very stern old boy, painfully short with most people, yet his long talks with Nick, boy and young man, had afforded him a great deal of pleasure. Girls were all very well, even exceedingly pretty little girls, but it was men who ruled the world, and here was young Nick McMasters born to be a leader. Colonel Parker's little legacy had helped a lot.

Dana bent her head over the album and her hair flowed around her. Yet her father had seen before she did that Nick wanted her. She simply had no idea of the passion in men's hearts. Her sheltered background had kept her peculiarly a child. Other girls her age had even borne a child, but she was still enmeshed in dreams, totally unprepared for conflict and a desperate, incomparable passion. She had been accustomed to seeing Nick as her wonderful big brother, the most brilliant, daredevil brother a girl ever had. The transition to lover broke up the known world—her world. The way life had been. She had never recovered.

Quietly Dana shut the album and put it away. Four years had passed since her father had been killed. Four years since Nick had forcibly been banished from her sight. She had to send him away—*had* to. To have run to him would have been to defeat her father, and death had done that. Between them they had stolen all her strength, denied her her own mind. She was more than just a prized possession. Nick had often said to her, *You belong to me*, caressing her soft skin, and later in their terrible arguments she had seethed at those very words. She wasn't going to be possessed, wrapped up and protected.

She was a person in her own right, a person with untapped potential.

In four years she'd had a lot of time to think about it. Enough time to discover herself, what was true. She had a successful business. Maybe she even had a husband if she wanted him. What she didn't have, finally, was freedom—freedom from Nick.

CHAPTER THREE

'WHAT are you going to do about Keith?' Vicki asked her.

It was afternoon of a beautiful spring Saturday and they were lazing beneath a majestic oak tree ringed by an arc of snowy azaleas. Two-year-old Timmy, fleetingly exhausted, was fast asleep with his amber head in his mother's lap, and not to be outdone Sheba, the family Labrador, had draped herself heavily across Dana's knees.

'What indeed?' Dana was automatically stroking behind the satin ears.

'He's a funny bloke!' Vicki sensed her friend's faintheartedness. 'Just between the two of us, I think he's a bit of a throwback to the Victorian male.'

'He wants to marry me,' said Dana.

'I figured he did.' Don't, *please*, Dana thought.

'I can't think marriage at all.'

'Of course not, love. You don't love him, that's all.'

'Have you ever thought I might finish up an old maid?' Dana asked her wryly. 'Aunty to Timmy and all the other children, none of my own?'

'I doubt that,' Vicki said firmly. 'The thing is, when are you going to train yourself to forget Nick?'

'I've been doing that for the last four years, I hope.'

'Except everything around here reminds you of

42

him. It would be nice if you could get away, though God knows I'd miss you.'

'Mm,' Dana murmured sceptically, and sighed. 'Changing my environment wouldn't help. I have to change myself inside. Some manage to rise above disastrous love affairs, but I can't shift Nick's image.'

'Can't or won't?' asked Vicki, sounding uneasy.

'How would you feel, Vicki, if you and Dave were forced into abandoning your marriage?'

Vicki didn't even have to consider. 'I'd feel shattered.'

'So it takes a long time to put the pieces back together.'

'For *you*,' Vicki burst out. 'Dana, I love you. We've always been the greatest friends, but not everyone has your capacity for feeling. You're an extraordinarily faithful person. Wonderfully loyal. Once it seemed to be that you and Nick shared some tremendous commitment to one another. Dave and I used to often ask ourselves what we were missing out on. No, don't look surprised. You and Nick had something not given to most of us, even to a couple as happy and as much in love as Dave and me. All of us felt the same—Bob and Kim, Sue and Darren. The way Nick used to look at you was enough to make any woman go shaky. He just consumed you with his eyes! He only had one mind—to get you. A lot of us made a pretty powerful play for him in the days when you were just a sweet little nun, but he just teased us deliberately, to show us he could have anyone if he wanted but he only wanted you. Don't fool yourself. I made a play for him myself. You weren't in love with him—you loved him. Then you suddenly woke up. Strange, any girl having filial thoughts about Nick—even on the TV the other night his sheer physicality blazed across. I mean, he's so blessed—that face, that body and all that brain thrown in. Dave actually taped the show so we could watch it again.'

'So?' Dana tilted back her head, knowing what Vicki was going to say before she said it.

'So maybe no man can be constant,' Vicki said gently. 'Don't let me hurt you, but it can't have escaped you Nick has been squiring around any number of women. Why, he was in the last issue of *Vogue*. The Holmans threw a big party, and who was there in all his magnificence but Nick, with Jan Holman on his arm? No gulf too broad for Nick to leap! From one of the poorest kids in this town to the top of the social tree. And if the way a girl clings to you is anything to go on, Jan Holman is definitely in love with him.'

'Which is only to be expected, I suppose. Don't worry, Vicki, I'm not jealous of the women in Nick's life. I have no right to be. I sent him away—relinquished him, if you like. I've seen the photographs in the magazines and the newspapers, and they tell their own story. Even so, falling out of love can be a very long process. We lose the people we love, we tend to build them an inner shrine. I'm parted from Nick on the outside, now I'm fighting him on the inside. I don't think he's ever really going to move out.' She gave Vicki a beautiful, heart-breaking smile. 'Terrible, isn't it? Like some terminal disease.'

'Damn it all, you've got no real men in your life.' Vicki scowled so she wouldn't cry. 'Keith is good-looking, successful, pretty well admired by everyone, but he's not what I want for you.

You're a sensitive soul, and every now and again I get the feeling that Keith isn't.'

'He can put things a little brutally,' said Dana.

'If you've discovered that, love, you can't let him into your life.'

'He has his good points.'

'Saints preserve us!'

'Then again, Vicki, he may be a little difficult to shake. Unfortunately he seems to have fallen rather violently in love with me, and it's typical of Keith to show tenacity.'

'In short, a dilemma?'

'Maybe the start of one,' Dana agreed. 'Why can't things stay the same? In the beginning Keith was very calm and controlled, but these days he's emotional as well. He's got some idea that I see myself as a statue on an altar and the only way he can free me is to rush me into bed.'

'At least he's normal!' Vicki gurgled, and started to laugh.

Timmy suddenly woke up, blinked, said: 'Hello!' then staggered to his feet.

'Now where are you off to, young man?' his mother asked him, her face so full of love it was almost beautiful.

'Play ball with Dana.' Timmy gestured towards a coloured rubber ball lying in the luxuriant, daisy-strewn grass.

'Duty calls.' Cued into it, Dana stood up. Sheba, the Labrador, was already braced into a waiting position. 'The next best thing in life to being Mamma is honorary Aunty.'

'He adores you,' said Vicki in her warm, vibrant voice. 'While you two are playing I'll get us a cold drink.'

Timmy threw the ball and automatically Sheba

dived on it, her waving tail expressing her immense enjoyment in the game. Dana sought to take the ball away from her, but she overrode it with an affected growl and bounded away, while Timmy ran hither and thither laughing and finally fell over.

The blessings of family life, Dana thought. There was absolutely nothing compared with a good marriage, children. Timmy was such a beautiful little boy, so merry and full of life he made her feel tremulous. Now he was up again, so Dana got her voice into the right Barbara Woodhouse register and commanded Sheba to return the ball.

'Twy clapping your hands, Dana,' Timmy urged her, pressing two fingers into his rosy, dimpled cheeks.

'I see what you mean.' Dana struck her hands together firmly and immediately Sheba trotted back with the ball and laid it at Dana's feet.

'Good girl!'

'Told you!' Timmy broke into a trill of laughter, to-ing and fro-ing as part of his strategy. 'Fwo it!'

Sheba quivered in anticipation, brown eyes like a lynx, so Dana pitched her hand one way, then quickly threw the ball another.

'Ooh!'

Sheba pounced.

Happy laughter drifted over the sweet-smelling, sun-filled garden. From her place in the kitchen, Vicki could see her beloved little boy, exuding the joy of childhood, Dana's slender, graceful figure chasing after Sheba. Both of them were being effortlessly out-manoeuvred by the exuberant Labrador.

'Sheba!' Vicki whistled and was ignored. Nine out of ten commands were totally ineffective with Sheba.

'Leave her. She's all right,' Dana called to her sweetly.

'Yeah, well ...'

Sheba, who positively adored Timmy, had now given him the ball.

Vicki smiled approvingly, then her beaming expression was replaced by one that was suddenly grim. Her throat tightened and her mouth pulled down at the corners. Ever since she could remember Dana had been known as the girl who had everything, the girl who could look forward to a wonderful life. People were always arrested by her radiant beauty, then found to their relief and pleasure that Dana was remarkably unassuming for one who had been given so much. Other rich girls were ghastly, but never Dana. As Dave, Vicki's husband, had been saying for years, Dana was one of the true aristocrats of this world. She *was*, yet life had played a cruel joke on her.

Vicki felt a lump rise in her throat as she looked out at her friend's moving figure, the sweep of one delicate, ivory cheek. She recalled Dana's father, Grant Merriman, a man greatly admired and respected, exclusive, like Dana, without being in the least snobbish. Certainly Vicki's own relatively modest background had not affected her friendship with Grant Merriman's only daughter. Grant Merriman had always been very kind to anyone who made his daughter happy. Except one.

It was odd really. Nick was now the millionaire, powerful and secure, while Dana was wandering around like a banished princess, a ghost of what she had been. Vicki's heart always ached when she thought about Dana and Nick. Once she would have sworn they shared a love on a plane few people aspired to, and yet after the ghastly episode of the engagement, some kind of feud had broken out. Both Dana and Nick had changed; Nick to become bitter and cynical, Dana to throw up an impenetrable reserve. There was no question Grant Merriman had pressured his daughter into giving Nick up, but Vicki, even in her loyalty, had always considered that Dana, for a girl so deeply in love, had surrendered her own claim to happiness far too easily. Nick's suffering had been acute and recognisable. Dana had simply—withdrawn. Grant Merriman had exerted his tremendous influence and Dana, like a dutiful daughter, had come to heel.

It wasn't an uncommon story. What had been uncommon was the extraordinary nature of the bond between Nick and Dana. It was a relationship their whole group had envied. Now the pathetic irony. All of them were happily married, or happy enough and Dana was the one left hungry for a love she had denied.

Vicki continued to stand at the kitchen sink, her hands arrested by her raging thoughts. What she had never known, what Grant Merriman had requested his daughter to withhold from everyone, was his heart condition. It was put as a little personal vanity, and afterwards, when Dana had the true version, she couldn't bring herself to tell anyone, even Vicki, of her father's betrayal. Even paternal love could be destructive.

For weeks, the subject that found its way into everyone's conversation was the company that had bought out Jim Stafford. Jim Stafford had never been the right owner for Merrilands, of course. The town and the vast surrounding district were in total agreement on that. Stafford wasn't one of the old Richmond families. Everyone knew the old Richmond families and everyone remembered Grant Merriman. Even though Jim Stafford had found the money to buy one of the finest properties in the rich sheep and wheat district the town had always considered him an outsider. Money, though part of being a member of the landed aristocracy, was by no means the main part. Jim Stafford and his wife had failed in every way, trying to buy favour, when the real families, like the Merrimans, had never had to do any such thing. Then again, Thea Stafford in her accumulative resentments had on at least two occasions aired her opinion of their own Dana Merriman, and the town had never forgiven her for that. It was outrageous that a travesty of a lady like Thea Stafford with a vocabulary rich in four-letter words should dare to criticise a very special person like Dana Merriman. Generations of good breeding had produced Dana when one could easily see Thea Stafford had brought herself up. The town was very hard on the Staffords.

Just when speculation and rumours were at their most rife, old Berny Starkey, who prided himself on knowing everything first, announced one morning to his serious drinking friends that 'a smashin' blonde had taken up residence at the Merrilands homestead'. She had driven up in a red Jaguar. He knew, because he had followed her. She was alone.

'The fancy lady of the new owner,' the regulars maintained.

Two days later Dana, in her capacity as interior decorator, was summoned to the house. She would have given anything to refuse, but as she was now a working girl that would have been excessively foolish. Still it would be a desperate effort maintaining her cool composure. Never a day passed that she didn't long to be back in her own home. Like her father she had loved Merrilands with a passion, at any rate on some level that made being away from it a kind of life sentence. The last four years had been a strange period, almost a contradiction. She had built up a successful business, yet so often her life seemed to her without motivation. At her lowest times, unendurable.

Aware that Jenny was staring at her, Dana caught herself up.

'What's she like?' Jenny suddenly cried, almost in desperation.

'Who, dear?'

'Why, the lady you were just speaking to. The lady at Merrilands.'

Dana rose and went mechanically to a row of luxurious new fabrics. 'I'm not wild about her.'

'I expect she's a real bitch.' Jenny nodded as though she understood.

'She did sound as though there was a vast difference between her and me.'

'She must be stinkin' rich,' Jenny observed.

'I would say so, Jenny.' Dana was still jarred by the rather metallic, lofty tone.

'One thing, she couldn't be worse than Mrs Stafford. Come to think of it, no one could be worse than Mrs Stafford. Do you remember that time she was booked for illegal parking? The air was *blue*!'

'Evidently her mother never washed her mouth out with soap.' Dana was only half following Jenny's chatter. 'I'm expected out there at two p.m. precisely.'

'Ooh, what an occasion!' Jenny giggled, then sobered. 'Are you sure you won't mind? I mean it's *your* house, isn't it?'

'How can it possibly be my house, Jenny?' Dana protested. 'I sold it, remember, for a very fair price.'

'And I'm sorry,' said Jenny, and for a few seconds tears stood in her eyes. 'Gran said you should never have had to part with your home.'

'Jenny, please.' Dana put her hand on the girl's shoulder. 'You and Gran are not to worry about me.'

'A lot of people worry about you,' Jenny returned. Which was quite true. In fact it often seemed anyone who bought Merrilands lost out on a lot of the town's good will.

'I can't understand why.' Dana gave the younger girl a long, amazed look. 'I have my health and strength. I'm not short of friends, *good* friends, or money.'

'It's sort of hard to explain.' With her right hand Jenny began to pick at a thread on a piece of curtaining material. 'You can't see yourself, I suppose.'

'I *can*.' Dana moved to a mirror and stared into it. 'That's a very self-possessed face.'

'It's your eyes,' Jenny told her. 'They look like they've been hurt. You've been hurt. It's the first thing anyone notices about you—your eyes. Even Dougie said to me you must have loved some guy very much.'

'Well then,' Dana murmured wryly, 'I'll have to take to wearing glasses.'

'Wouldn't matter if you did,' Jenny maintained, still pulling at the thread dejectedly. 'Gran told me they had to put Nick McMasters in jail one time to calm him down. Gran said he was crazy when he had to let you go.'

'Gran's a romantic, Jenny, and so are you. Anyway, it's a long time ago.' Dana spoke quietly, hiding behind a well established, poised manner. 'You've got your pad there, Jenny, haven't you? I want you to jot down a few things. If we're to refurbish Merrilands, I imagine it will be a big job.'

'What if she doesn't like our taste?' Jenny considered, very logically.

'Then we'll have to rush away in great haste. They can always bring in one of the smart decorators from Sydney. In fact, now that I think about it, I fail to see why they've summoned me.'

'Because you're marvellous with old houses,' Jenny told her in a rush. 'Gran says it's because you were used to so much gracious living.' Dana was silent so Jenny went on. 'Most of us grew up in houses that would fit into your sitting room.'

'I shouldn't worry about size, if I were you,' Dana said impassively. 'What does it matter how big a house is if the people who live in it are happy?'

'Because, Miss Merriman, if the house is too small you go mad. And it doesn't do much for artistic creativity either. I reckon you know how to do up things because once you were really rich. You had lots of things to move about. On the other hand, Gran and I have only a few old battered things to bang together. There's no chance to develop an eye.'

'Then that solves what I'm going to give you

and Gran for Christmas. What about a nice large sofa so you can be comfortable watching television?'

'A *sofa*?' Jenny was in a quandary. A sofa would be nice, but so were other things. She wanted time to think.

Dana looked up, registering Jenny's faintly agonised expression. 'Anyway, you have plenty of time to think about it.'

'Gran's already started on your present,' said Jenny. 'I can't tell you what it is, but you're going to love it.'

'I'm sure I shall.' Dana was touched.

'And what's the name of the odious, stuck-up lady on the phone?'

'Jenny!'

'Oh, I won't say that to anyone else,' Jenny giggled. 'I've learnt a little about diplomacy since I started to work for you.'

'I suppose so,' Dana agreed rather feebly.

'So what's her name?'

'Curiously she didn't say, and I wasn't one bit surprised. No doubt she didn't want to load me down with too many details.'

'But that's odd.' Jenny shook her chestnut head.

'Certain pompous people like to put the workers in their place. She merely said she was speaking from Merrilands. I'd been recommended and would I please call.'

'What happens if you didn't?'

'We'd probably lose out on a lot of money.' Dana caught up her car keys and slipped them into her handbag.

'Probably after this afternoon she'll be begging you to help her,' Jenny said happily. 'You look and act so exactly right.'

'Bless you, Jenny, for those kinds words. Let's hope the mysterious mistress of Merrilands looks at me the same way!'

Yet it was apprehension that rode along with Dana like a prickling at the nape of her neck. It was a full thirty minutes' drive out to the station, past rippling oceans of golden wheat. In a week or two it would be ready for harvest. She could almost feel the break of the ripe, dry kernels on her teeth. It was beautiful country she was driving through, the roadway and the surrounding hills glorious with blossom, from the lavender blue of the jacarandas through the showy pinks of the almond and peach to the gold of the wattles that filled the air with such fragrance. Woolly white new lambs were out in the paddocks where thousands of yellow and white daisies grew wild. Sheep and cattle were grazing on the slopes and horses stood cropping in paddocks lush with verdure. She almost reeled under the memory of other springs. So many perfect, beautiful times. It was spring when she and Nick had become engaged and for at least a few days she had come closer to perfect happiness than perhaps mortal woman was allowed.

She was still driving her father's expensive car, a Daimler Van den Plas. No one, including herself, saw anything incongruous in it. Other people could get away with an economical little runabout, not Dana Merriman. She could never escape being a Merriman even when her whole world had come tumbling down.

Ten minutes later she turned into the private road that meandered through the fertile valley occupied by the still magnificent property of

Merrilands. Her grandfather had always said there was gold on it; not the gold of the great wheat paddocks or the blazing bursts of wattle but the precious metal that had brought prospectors from all parts of the world to the Australian gold-fields in the 1800s. But where other men were possessed by gold fever, John Henry Merriman, her great-great-grandfather, had been possessed by the land, of building a mansion-homestead, of breeding the finest strain of merinos in the land. By the time her great-grandfather was a young man there was no finer property than Merrilands in the whole colony. Merrilands wool. Merrilands horses. The breeding of fine horses had been very much a part of the old Merrilands. They had never bred a Melbourne Cup winner, but a Merrilands-bred thoroughbred had carried off many another prestigeous cup. She still had their collection of thoroughbred paintings intact. All their great champions had been painted, adorning the walls of the library and the study, in the Merrilands that was.

On foot, the journey towards the homestead would have seemed endless. Even on horseback it was quite a ride, but the Daimler made nothing of distance, and suddenly it was there, a splendid colonial mansion, Georgian in style. A great house of mellow, rose-hued brick with white pillars rising to a verandahed upper story enclosed in superb white wrought-iron lace. There were other buildings behind it and ranged on either side, but even if they hadn't been all but hidden in their oasis of trees nothing could have distracted the eye from the homestead itself.

Dana stopped the car in the shade of one of the

countless blossoming jacarandas and switched off the ignition. The double doors with their beautiful fanlights and sidelights of stained glass were wide open but there was no sign of life. Dana mounted the short flight of stone steps without hurry, the very picture of cool elegance, her spirits wavering inside. Merrilands was precious to her, for all it was full of ghosts.

Another shivery thought. Someone was watching her, had been watching her for some time. The desire to lift her eyes to the upper storey was very strong, but she resisted it. She put her hand to the doorbell listening to its melodious peal, but nothing moved. Something else was bewildering her. The beautiful wide entrance hall looked terrible. Mustard-coloured carpet covered the beautifully patterned tiled floor, the gleaming woodwork had been painted and the mouldings of the elaborate plasterwork with Corinthian-capped half columns, picked out in an assortment of colours that offended her eye. The magnificent Persian runner they had left on the centrally placed staircase had been replaced by the same mustard carpeting and the light-bearing classical bronzes removed from their century-long role of guarding the great stairway. All that remained untouched was the great stained glass window on the first landing, and even its surrounding woodwork had been covered with cream paint. It would be an enormous job getting all that paint off. Keith had told her the Staffords had made 'a hash' of redecorating, but this was far worse than she had imagined. How could anyone in their right mind cover up the tiled floor? It made no sense at all.

Dana was just deciding to ring the doorbell

again when a voice reached her from the upper level.

'One moment, please.'

It sounded languid yet indignant, as though the owner disdained answering doorbells. Dana tried to remain unaffected, her violet eyes looking upwards towards the landing where the staircase divided into two. She fully expected to see a handsome, rather difficult woman turn into sight, but not the dynamic creature who now faced her with the magnificent stained glass window as a backdrop.

For one thing, she was younger than her rather deeply modulated voice had suggested. Twenty-eight, thirty, it was hard to tell. She stood, tall, bone-thin, a frozen image from one of the glossy fashion magazines, her hair in stunning contrast to her yellow silk shirt, a radiant rich red.

'Good afternoon,' Dana said pleasantly, trying not to stare. 'I'm Dana Merriman.'

'I should hope so!' the other returned forcefully. 'No one else has been invited here.'

It was the oddest greeting Dana had ever had, but now the woman was moving down the stairway, expressing with an imperious gesture of her hand that Dana should come right on in.

'Fascinating, isn't it?' she said, glancing around. 'I gather the last owners didn't quite live up to the locals' expectation of them. Whoever picked the colour scheme must have been an idiot.'

Dana agreed, but did not reply. Close to she could see that that glorious mane wasn't natural, unless there existed the redhead with black brows, dark brown eyes and olive skin. So many women coloured their hair these days, and Dana had to admit this woman carried off the colour change quite magnificently. The bright hair fell back from a strongly boned, mocking face, and her dark eyes glittered against smooth olive skin. She wasn't beautiful but striking. The tall figure was almost breastless, hipless. She would have made a perfect model.

'Well, come in. Come in.'

'Thank you.' Dana glanced towards her. 'I didn't catch your name over the phone.'

'I'm not surprised, I never gave it.'

'But you will now.'

'Aren't you the hoity-toity one!' the redhead laughed. 'I guess you sort of cultivate it in your business.'

'I would like know to whom I'm speaking,' Dana returned mildly.

'Good for you! I'm Jay Benson. I don't own this place, not yet, anyway, but I've been told to engage you by the owner who prefers to remain anonymous for the time being. It's the best guarantee for a bit of peace.'

'I can appreciate that,' said Dana when what she really meant was—why add to the confusion? 'May I ask who recommended me?' she added simply.

'Andrea . . . Andrea someone.'

'Andrea Schofield?'

'Isn't it awful? I can't remember.' The redhead wrapped herself into an armchair with a grace so feline it was something to watch. 'Anyway, it's not important. I'm to offer you a very important job—redecorate this place. As you can see what has been done is pretty awful. Personally, I think these huge old places are obsolete, hopeless in terms of easy living and maintenance.'

Dana could not control her flash of anger, though her voice remained quiet. 'It's one of the finest historic homesteads in the country.'

'Oh, yes, quite.' Jay Benson gave the impression she was most amused. 'I expect *you* like it?'

Suddenly it occurred to Dana that the young woman who faced her had no idea of Dana's background or the fact that this was her old family home. 'I love it,' she confirmed.

'Ah well, as they say, each to her own poison. As far as I'm concerned the glorious days of the homesteaders are over.'

'Certainly many of the great properties have been broken up,' Dana agreed, 'but houses like these are doubly valuable to us. They're part of our short heritage. The men that built these houses built Australia. The homestead is as important to us as the grandest English castle is to an Englishman, or indeed all of us, for that matter. The man who built this house was an Englishman.'

'Isn't that jolly?' Jay Benson gave her a mocking, sidelong glance. 'All for the honour and glory of the Empire, of course.'

'Yes, thank God!' Dana said it with more asperity than she intended, and the mocking look left the redhead's face altogether. Little sparks of antagonism had ignited, almost ready to flame. It couldn't be allowed to happen in the name of good manners and plain economics. 'Shall I be meeting with the owner?' Dana asked in a purposefully tranquil voice. 'I always make a practice of sitting down with my clients and discussing all the details first. There must be a feeling of appropriateness, of course, in houses like these. . . .'

'You have a knowledge of period, have you?' Jay Benson had obviously decided she didn't have to be careful, for her tone was sharp to the point of rudeness.

'I would know how to handle this house, yes.'

'Well, I've been led to believe you're very good, which apparently has nothing to do with the fact that you choose to operate in a virtual backwater. What are your qualifications?'

For an instant Dana found herself sick in the stomach. All of her clients showed her the utmost friendliness and courtesy, so it wasn't easy to deal with antagonism and challenge. She sat a little straighter, her white skin turned to marble. 'I haven't a string of diplomas, Miss Benson, if that's what you mean. Yet it's not extraordinary for a woman with certain natural gifts to become a very successful designer. Some of the most admired and influential decorators of the past were women with no formal training.'

'I don't need to be told that.' There was a decided glint in the bright dark eyes. 'But those women usually came from a world vastly different from your own. Interior decorating, you might say, was only a hobby, something to fill in the time between brilliant house parties. They were women of wealth and aristocratic backgrounds.'

'Not all, but certainly they were women of taste and breeding. For myself, Miss Benson, all I can tell you is, *you* asked *me* here to Merrilands. This may be a country town, but I do have an impressive number of clients, all of whom are doing splendidly. I've never worked where my surroundings or my clients haven't been harmonious, so if you have any doubts at all, I shan't waste any more of our time.'

It wasn't until Dana was standing that she realised the redhead was staring at her in some surprise. 'You're very touchy, aren't you?'

'I don't think so,' Dana tried a pleasant smile. 'But I know you will appreciate that I can only work with a certain kind of client, preferably where we see things in much the same way. I have no desire whatever to impose my taste on my clients, but rather to work together to produce the best possible design for a particular residence and lifestyle. I suppose I'm merely an interpreter and a guider at times. The end result, I always hope, is quality.'

'And I'm sure you achieve it,' Jay Benson murmured, with a gleam of maliciousness. 'Do please sit down again, I hate talking to people when they're standing on their dignity.'

And you must do a lot of it, Dana thought, but didn't say. It was obvious now that Jay Benson had disliked her at first sight, which was a little unusual, because she wasn't normally disliked. Probably she wanted to do the place over herself or at least bring in her own decorator, but the owner had apparently been uncompromising in his selection. As soon as she got back to the shop she would ring Andrea Schofield and gently ask a few questions.

'I think it extremely brave myself,' Jay Benson was now saying, one long thin hand to her luxuriant mane, 'but I've been instructed by the owner to offer you carte blanche. You're to do everything you see fit with a virtually unlimited budget. In other words, you have a free rein.'

It was far from what Dana wanted, yet from

the expression on Jay Benson's face it was obvious she thought Dana had been offered the commission of a lifetime.

'And I'm to have no intimation whatever of the owner's personal tastes?'

'I agree it doesn't make perfect sense.' The redhead stifled the faintest yawn.

'And what about lifestyle? Is this to be a permanent residence?'

'A getaway, rather.'

'A *getaway*?' Dana couldn't have been more shocked or dismayed. Properties, a working property like Merrilands, could not be used as a 'getaway'.

'Another thing,' the redhead informed her, 'a new manager is arriving in a day or so—a replacement for the old chap that was here. Be assured the property will continue to be run as a sheep station, but entirely more successfully than it has been. When you've finished the ground floor of the house, the master bedroom suite and several bedrooms as guest rooms you can turn your attention to the manager's residence if you want. There will be a housekeeper brought in here and her caretaker husband, and in the next few weeks gardeners and whatever workmen you need. The house and its surrounding garden acres are to be brought very much to a high standard of excellence.'

'And I can act entirely as I wish?'

'You don't seem happy with it, Miss Merman.' There was a certain pleasure in the redhead's voice. 'If you were to think it too big a job I'm certain I understand. I could even tell the owner today that the answer is no. I admit you're talented, but I don't imagine you've handled another commission on this scale?'

Why don't I just say I used to live here? Dana thought. Why don't I say my name is Merriman, not Merman? It was extraordinary, the whole thing.

'Don't look so worried,' said Jay Benson. 'One needs to have a great deal of confidence to handle the refurbishing of a place like this, and I don't imagine you've had the time or the experience to acquire it. You can't be more than twenty-three or four?' The dark eyes were hard on Dana as she spoke.

'Twenty-six.'

'Is *that* what you are! The owner must be dreaming to give you the commission. This isn't my style of house, far from it, but I daresay I could have taken charge quite as well as you.'

'Did you not suggest it?' Dana asked.

'I did, of course, but apparently ...' a few seconds while she swallowed the name on the tip of her tongue '... the owner, my friend, had heard about the work you were doing. I can correct his impression, if you like. Personally I think it ridiculous to offer such a big job to so young a woman.'

'The size of the job doesn't worry me,' Dana assured her.

'I'm amazed at your conviction.'

'Doesn't my name mean anything to you, Miss Benson?' Dana asked.

'Your name? Oh, come on, you're kidding me. Are you someone important in disguise?'

'Not important but familiar with Merrilands,' said Dana. She looked away for a moment over the beautifully proportioned drawing room. The wonderful moiré antique paper, white with a tiny pattern of gold, had been replaced by a floral print more suited to a bedroom, and she gazed at it rather helplessly. 'Perhaps I should have corrected you before. My name isn't Merman, but Merriman.'

'What the hell!' the redhead laughed, a shade uneasily. 'Should I grasp something from that?'

Dana smiled wryly. 'Only that I'm used to a house this size. In fact, I'm used to *this* house. I was born here.'

'I don't believe it!' The older woman stared at her aghast.

'I'm surprised you don't know. Surely it came out at some time? Andrea Schofield would certainly have mentioned me in connection with the house. Everyone in this district knows me, knows all about the Merrimans. I had to sell the property after my father was killed.'

'My God!' There was no sympathy in the nearly savage exclamation, only a kind of anger. 'I wonder if all this was reported?'

'What, to the owner?'

'Certainly the owner.' Jay Benson gave her a pretty formidable glance. 'Everything points to some kind of conspiracy.'

'I assure you, *no*.' Dana didn't even flush under the curiously angry gaze. 'For one thing, no one in the district knows the identity of the owner or even his company name. In a way it's a little bizarre, like Howard Hughes.'

'Rich men do things *their* way,' Jay Benson told her. It was obvious she was still greatly shaken by Dana's identity. 'Perhaps if you can keep this to yourself for a day or two, you'll hear more.'

'If that's what you want.' This time Dana definitely intended to leave. 'We'll be in contact, then, shall we? I have rather a lot to do, so I'll take myself off.'

Dana's tall, slender frame moved with ease through her familiar surroundings and, looking at her, Jay Benson experienced a rare upsurge of bitterest jealousy. To begin with, she had never thought to meet anyone remotely like Dana in a country town. It still amazed her how any small-time decorator could look so good. Her posture was perfect, grooming impeccable, yet she appeared unaware of her own beauty. She wore a superb white linen suit with a black trim and her black shoes and bag were definitely Italian. It was really absurd. What should have been a push-over had turned out to be heavy weather.

'Didn't I say at the beginning you fell into the hoity-toity bracket?' Jay commented contemptuously, otherwise there was no coping with this quality of grace.

'That is never my intention.' A faint blush moved into Dana's creamy cheeks, but she gave no other sign that she was upset by the other's unpleasantness. 'I'll say goodbye then, Miss Benson.'

'Yes, goodbye.' It was a dismissal and a curt one. 'You needn't consider you have the job until you hear from me again.'

'Of course.' Dana inclined her gleaming raven head. Such an unfolding of antagonism was beginning to mean less and less to her. She was moving through a haze of memories, some happy, some too unbearably sad. She could almost see her father standing across the room and she turned away quickly before her violet eyes filled with tears. Though she believed in her heart that her father had injured her she could never think of him without wanting to cry. Once they had been gloriously happy until Nick had become the object of her love, but the bond between parent and child was so extraordinary nothing could ever wholly undermine it.

Dana walked slowly to the front door as though she expected at every step that a beloved voice would call her. It would be a relief to miss out on the job—a blessed, blessed relief. The golden days of Merrilands had long since passed away. Jay Benson would have no difficulty persuading her friend, the owner, to try somebody else.

Sunlight burst over Dana like a waterfall, and looking away over the parklike vista of the four acres of home garden, the lyrical beauty of spring, she was suddenly overcome by a melancholia that threatened to destroy the quietness of spirit she had so sternly cultivated. For all her determination, her memories were more positive than her real life.

CHAPTER FOUR

EVEN as Dana went to press the front doorbell, Mrs Owens, Merriland's new housekeeper, hurried out to meet her.

'Good morning, dear.'

Dana gave her a smile of equal warmth. 'How are you, Mrs Owens? I haven't seen the grounds looking so lovely in a long time.'

Mrs Owens' round, cheerful face went pink with pleasure. 'Bill will appreciate that, dear. Coming from *you*.'

'Then certainly I'll tell him as well.'

'Oh, he loves working about the place,' Mrs Owens declared comfortably, sweeping some non-existent dust from the door-jamb. 'By the way, dear,' she said with a lowered tone and glittering eyes, 'we're to expect our employer some time this morning.'

'Not the legendary Mr M.?' Dana was so surprised she nearly jumped. 'When did you hear this?'

'Bill took the call late last night.' Mrs Owens' second chin quivered. 'I was asleep at the time, so he only told me this morning. I've been on the go ever since.'

'No wonder!' Dana followed the housekeeper's ample form as she led the way into the house. 'This is a great occasion.'

'It shocked me as well.' Mrs Owens looked back and rolled her eyes. 'What do you say we have a cup of tea to revive us?'

'Lovely.' For a moment Dana stood anxiously, surveying her handiwork. For the past month she and her team of helpers had laboured exhaustively to work a transformation, or rather restore the house to what it once had been, but when one didn't have the presence or the co-operation of the client it was very much like working in the dark. More than half the satisfaction of the job was working in close harmony with the owner, planning together what they wanted to achieve, but there had been none of that at Merrilands. She had worked alone with nothing else in mind than that her mysterious client, Mr and Mrs Owen's 'Mr M.' was a very wealthy bachelor. Jay Benson, who had never contacted her again, could be one of many women friends for all Dana knew and her specific instructions seemed to suggest this, for she had been bound to no one one else's taste but her own.

'Now, now, dear,' Mrs Owens, seeing she was anxious, became bracingly supportive. 'Don't you go fretting about what he's going to say. The place is a picture—something right out of a film or some of those magazines you leave about the place—*Architectural Digest*. I've never been in a lovelier house in my life, and we've worked in some pretty swish places, I can tell you. This is different. It's a real home with a history.'

'Let's hope your Mr M. likes what I've done,' Dana said nervously. 'I have a peculiar feeling about him.'

'He couldn't help but like it,' Mrs Owens declared. 'I mean, he bought it the way it was. Who would ever have thought of covering up those glorious tiles with carpet? And that funny murky shade? Why, every time I walk through the hall now I think of beautiful autumn leaves.'

'Um.' Dana wandered back into the entrance hall, tracing the mosaic design of the tiles with the elegant point of her shoe. They did have the rich colours of autumn leaves, with touches of blue. French polishers had restored the gleaming woodwork, the plastered walls returned to an eggshell blue and the elaborate mouldings picked out in a magnolia white and gold. The Persian runner, miraculously intact in one of the store rooms, had been very carefully cleaned and returned to the staircase, and she had successfully negotiated the purchase of Merrilands' old bronzes to accentuate the beautiful symmetry of the grand, centrally placed stairway.

'Bill thinks you're something of a genius,' Mrs Owen's confided. 'I mean, you're so young, yet you're able to take on redecorating a great house like this.'

'Maybe it's because I know every inch of it,' Dana answered promptly. 'Did he say anything about me? How am I getting on? Did he like what I'm doing? *Anything?*'

'I'm afraid I didn't question Bill very closely,' said Mrs Owens, and patted Dana's arm cosily. 'But my goodness, dear, you have nothing to worry about. Everything you've done looks lovely and comfortable and just right. It's a real home, if you know what I mean. Some places you're frightened to sit down, but— valuable antiques nevertheless—you'd never be frightened to sit down here. If you want to know, I'm looking forward to hearing him tell you you've done wonders.' Her manner suggested she would gladly resign if he didn't.

Grateful for so much friendly support, Dana immediately felt better. 'Well, it was his own idea in any case to allow me full control. I was having some workmen in today. Do you think I should put them off?'

'Oh, *I* would,' Mrs Owens said briskly. 'Then you can talk quietly.'

'That's if he's come to talk to me at all. Probably he wants to talk to Mr Steele.'

'*You*, actually,' Mrs Owens murmured, then looked slightly alarmed. 'I'll go off and make that cup of tea.'

'Did he mention no set time?' Dana called after her, feeling vaguely uneasy.

'I expect we'll have to keep ourselves at the ready all day,' Mrs Owens replied jovially. 'We're lucky, I suppose, we got a few hours' advance warning.'

'Warning' was the operative word, Dana thought, and turned back to her inspection of the completed rooms. It was true she had worked very hard. 'Like a slave,' Keith had grumbled in one of his bad moods. The results to her eye were very rewarding—a graceful mix of classic, antique furnishings with plump modern sofas. The white and gold wallpaper in the drawing room, a copy of a beautiful early nineteenth-century design, had been fearfully expensive but necessary to hold its own against the richly gilded ceiling, and she had already started an Italian master craftsman on the restoration work on the coffered ceiling in the library. Or the library that was. It was not possible to dwell on what had happened to the magnificent bookcases that had flanked the fireplace and lined the west wall. The multitudes of leather bound books, apart from a trunkload of

Dana's favourites, had been scooped up avidly by collectors, otherwise they might have finished up on a bonfire.

The dining room had presented few problems. She had found exactly what she wanted there, but today it was taking her an amazingly long time to see what she wanted to do with the room the family had always called the Chinese Room. Once it had housed a formidable assemblage of Chinese art and antiques, but after the BASCO crash her father had sold it for a fabulous price to a well-known Hong Kong collector. The Staffords, however, had stripped it of an exceptionally fine chinoiserie paper and lacquered the walls in a more lively shade of fire-engine red.

Of course, as the owners they were entitled to do as they liked, but Dana had found herself doing an extraordinary amount of private wailing at their radical departure from traditional formal grace. It was almost as though they had deliberately set out to turn an unusually grand colonial homestead into an amusing rustic retreat. Some sort of game had caused the bullet hole in the central panel of the library ceiling, she was sure. Keith had told her it had been appealingly decorated with heads from several African safaris. Jim Stafford had been an enthusiastic big game hunter until apparently a near-miss cured him.

Her thoughts seemed to be moving off in all directions. It was the worst possible commission to be given carte blanche. Supposing he should come in and say: 'My God, you'll have to do this all over again!' Jim Stafford had certainly said it to his wife. Not everyone shared the Merriman taste in interior design which was basically, given a place like Merrilands, English country house.

The Staffords had wasted little time stripping it of all those elements. Perhaps the mysterious Mr M. was just such a person. Never mind her father would have called him a 'barbarian', he was her client and she had already spent a good deal of his money.

The day wore on and Dana concerned herself with taking measurements and making sketches, juggling this idea against that. If she knew precisely what kind of man she was dealing with ... his attitudes, interests, his plans for the house, what kind of entertaining he was going to do, on what scale? Surely he planned to spend a good deal of time here. The most beautiful house had to be lived in, otherwise it became lifeless. Many times, Dana shook her head and sighed aloud. Was it possible he was only doing the house up to resell the property? Millionaires were always concerned with making money. There was no use asking Bruce Steele, Merrilands' new manager. Nice as he was, he was remarkably close-lipped about the company that employed him.

The most extraordinary thing about the Staffords was that they had left several valuable antique fixtures in the attic, a very beautiful porcelain chandelier that had once graced a bedroom, the huge gilded mirror from the old ballroom and the Persian runner from the staircase. Had they no idea of the value of such things, or had they so much money they were totally unconcerned? Perhaps she should check on exactly what was there, since she intended to return at least a few pieces to their rightful place.

Before going up to the attic she looked about for Mrs Owens, but there was no sign of her.

Perhaps she had gone out into the garden to have a word with her husband. Dana smiled as she thought of capable, kind Bill. Obviously their odd employer had taken no gamble on *them*. Not only were they both extremely efficient but they had a genuine love for the property they were caretaking. Dana had taken to them both at once, and it was true they liked her, showing it in all kinds of ways.

The attic, in fact, resembled some fantastic junk shop, where here and there a valuable antique was crowded or half covered by a variety of rather nightmarish ultra-modern furnishings even the Staffords had become bored with. Dana had to edge herself around, for although the attic was shut up dust still blew through minute cracks around the window, settling comfortably on everything it could reach. She wasn't really dressed for exploring, neither was it the day for it. Decorators were supposed to be serious about their appearance, and keeping dust off virgin white was a problem.

It was becoming very hot and even with the door open Dana realised she would have to open the window. It gave after several hard pushes and as the breeze gusted in, the attic door blew shut. No matter. Dana raised her head abruptly, looking up into the densely blue sky where a twin-engined light aircraft was quickly losing altitude, aiming for the station runway.

So Mr M. was arriving by plane. Normally she wasn't the least nervous of meeting clients or new people, but a peculiar tension like a thin line of blue fire was eating slowly along her veins. Dana continued to stare out while the aircraft, a Beech Baron, she could see that now, made its approach. A few moments later it was lost through the trees.

She swung about and as she did so she caught her reflection in one end of the huge giltwood mirror that had graced the ballroom for more than a hundred years. It gave her an even stranger sensation to see herself so presented. In fact it was almost a shock like encountering a stranger. Against the gleaming blackness of her hair, her skin looked very white, exaggerated again by the delicate black wings of her brows and the dark density of her eyelashes. With this heightened clarity of sensation, perception, she wasn't surprised to see her eyes looked huge and troubled, clouded with little apprehensions she now tried to shake off. A quick glance down assured her her sleeveless slim-line white crêpe-de-chine dress was still dazzlingly clean and she was able to move towards the door. In all probability he was being met by the manager, in which case they should arrive at the house within five or ten minutes.

Something she had not noticed before now forcibly struck her eyes. There was no knob on the door. She glanced around the floor expecting to find it there, then she shifted her frowning stare back to the brass shaft. Perhaps she could manage to turn it with one of the pins from her hair? She would certainly have to try or start screeching for help. How delighted Jay Benson would be to catch her out in such a silly position!

She lost a little more time searching around for the knob, but it was clear it had not recently fallen off. As the door had always been in good repair she had never suspected she might be shut in, and she bit her lip in nervous strain.

Her hairpins were all too fine for the screwhole, so she unbuckled the wide belt at her waist, between one thing and another on the point of hammering at the door like a frightened child.

This was ridiculous, and she realised now that she would never get out unless she called for help. It would require all her lung power and even then she had no confidence that she would be heard. It was a very large house and she was right at the top of it. If only she had told Mrs Owens where she was going!

After a further twenty minutes of calling and knocking she knew she was trapped until finally a search of the house led someone to the attic. She didn't even care now about her dress, moving back to sit down on a very old, spindly chair. She had bent so many of her hairpins her long hair was now brushing her face and her normally cool skin was flushed with heat and an agitation out of all proportion to her mild dilemma. Her car was still parked in the drive, so of course she had to be somewhere in the house. Mrs Owens, most likely, would find her. She couldn't even rouse herself to shout once more. She had simply to wait.

Minutes more passed and she began to see herself beating both fists against the stout wooden door. From time to time she had gone to the window to look out, but she was facing a section of the garden where no one was working. She sat down again shakily, trying to dismiss a touch of pure panic. Now the smell of dust, old fabrics and furniture was overpowering, and in a total absence of mind she traced interlocking initials in the dust of a small rosewood table. A flowing D. and an N.

'My God!' she murmured aloud. She was almost in tears.

Footsteps rushing up the winding stairs calmed her and she stared fixedly at the doorshaft waiting for it to turn. Her hands still smarted and her throat hurt as if she had been crying violently. For someone who was expecting to see the comforting presence of Mrs Owens she found she was shaking all over, so unlike her normal self, reality seemed distorted. What a very small thing to get into such an overwrought state about, yet her sensitive emotional antennae were picking up warning vibrations. She had good reason to believe in her own intuitions, the indefinable sensations that told her something was very wrong.

It had flashed into her mind that her father was dead several hours before the fatal accident was confirmed. Other things too. She had never known why she had premonitions. It was simply a fact. Even when she had been so magically happy with Nick she had known it would very soon end.

Nick.

She flung up her head in a strained, listening attitude as though she could hear him calling her from some distance. She had to be a little crazy, because she had the impression he was coming near. Her own loss of control shocked her. She, the cool one, locked in some continuing, hopeless fantasy. Yet the more she pushed the idea away, the closer he came.

It was the heat and the closeness, the faint claustrophobia that sometimes haunted her. It would be so easy sometimes to give oneself up to hysteria.

The door flew back violently and as Dana started up she thought she really had gone out of her mind. She actually cried out, bringing up a hand across her eyes.

'No, *no*!' She was gasping for breath.

'Stop that.' His black eyes were fixed on her with the same magnetic force.

'So it *is* you.' Her slender body crumpled and she yielded to soft, helpless laughter. 'My God!'

His voice cut in coldly. 'You'd better come out of here, don't you think?'

'Oh, why not!' She couldn't check the desperate laughter, and he caught her uplifted arm at the elbow.

'Steady! Surely my appearance can't affect you so insanely?'

'Even when we were children you used to frighten me,' she whispered raggedly.

'Really? I thought you were devoted to me.' His tightening grip had a touch of cruelty. 'It *is* over, Dana. I *am* here, and I own Merrilands.'

'Yes.' She was just managing not to faint. 'Daddy always said you had too much ambition.'

'*Daddy* always said you would never marry me.'

They were staring full into each other's eyes.

Oh, God, give me strength, Dana prayed. I've got to pretend to be strong.

He looked like a heathen, a pirate that could take and break anything he desired. Gone was the sweetness, the smile she would die for, and in its place a look of steel that was beyond her.

'Did you never even guess at the truth?' he said harshly.

'Would I be here if I did?'

'I would like to know.'

'Never.' Dana shook her head dazedly.

'And now that you do know?'

'I can hardly continue.'

'You'd dismiss a contract?' he asked with incredible smoothness.

'I would never have considered it had I known it was you Nick.'

He was still gripping her arm, yet he seemed unaware of it. 'Hence this elaborate charade. Doesn't it seem unbelievable that I've won this great prize?'

'You always loved power,' she said, her throat pulled tight.

'Agreed.' The curvy mouth twisted beneath the black, rakish moustache. 'Once I even loved you. But that was another lifetime.'

Dana didn't answer, neither could she sustain the too-nakedly contemptuous, brilliant look.

The breeze came again in an erratic gust, and as once before, the attic door slammed shut.

Dana flung her arms around her, wincing at the sound. 'I believe we're locked in again!' she exclaimed with that same little touch of hysteria.

'Locked in?' Nick released her abruptly and turned. 'I'm much too clever to be trapped anywhere.'

'Your *cleverness* was never in question, Nick.'

'Do you *want* me to rescue you?'

She felt the colour moving under her cheeks. 'Go ahead.'

'Yes. Yes, of course, Miss Merriman.' There was anger, terrible anger behind the suave mockery. He knelt down and the muscles rippled the thin cloth of his shirt. He had always had a magnificent body, not the lean elegance of the clothes-horse, but flauntingly male; powerful shoulders and broad chest tapering away to a narrow waist and sleek flanks. He looked much more the professional athlete than a man who had made a fortune in space-age technology.

'Can you do it?' she asked quietly as he jiggled keys and a few gadgets on his key-ring.

'Does it matter if we get locked in?'

'Why should it matter any more?'

The shaft turned noiselessly and a moment later he stood up and opened the door wide. 'Never mind all the money you're spending, this door could do with a new lock.'

'I never noticed when I came in.' With a supreme effort she tried to act naturally, but she was too greatly affected to carry it off.

'Are you going to come out?'

'Of course.' Her face was colourless except for her violet eyes and glowing mouth. 'I'm still recovering from the shock.'

'You were never very brave.'

She moved towards him, seeing the tautness come into his face. 'You planned this, Nick. All of it?'

'In every trival aspect. Except for locking you in.'

'And you expect me to go on with this ... impossible commission?'

He bowed slightly. 'I'm looking forward to ensuring you do.'

'You're mad!' She couldn't stop the words fluttering from her mouth.

'Come,' his black eyes narrowed, *you're* the one who gave way to hysteria.'

Her hand came up to touch her quivering mouth. 'I've had the oddest feeling all day.'

'Of course, you always were super-sensitive. In some things.'

His antagonism was so great she had to recoil against the wall. 'I can't stay, Nick.'

'Don't talk like a child.' His dark face was set and ruthless, the skin golden, clenched teeth very white. 'You accepted a commission, remember? Signed a contract. I'd advise you not to try to get out of it.'

'Nick . . . *please*!'

He sucked in his breath. 'Could the exquisite Miss Merriman be begging?'

'Why should I have to?'

'I expect it's all part of my little revenge.' He smiled down at her, mocking her, the striking, bold face almost sinister.

'Daddy always said you could be cruel,' she said bitterly.

Nick moved so swiftly, he shocked her, pinning her against the wall. 'Don't you ever want to grow up?'

'I'm twenty-six years old,' Dana reminded him.

'What the hell! You're still Grant Merriman's little girl.'

'So I've got a tag on me.'

'Yes.' He caught her face between his hands, forcing up her head. 'I want to look at you.'

'Please. Oh, please, Nick!' She just had to shut her eyes.

'Your father was my worst enemy,' he grated.

'No, Nick, don't say that!'

His brief laugh was full of irony. 'Darling, even you can't deny it. Open your eyes.'

'I think if I do, you might kill me.'

'I might have, once. But that's in the past. My miserable, blighted, unforgettable past.'

'Don't let it hurt you, Nick,' she said. 'You're no longer. . . .'

'A nobody?'

She turned her head desperately. 'I wasn't going to say that.'

'What *were* you going to say, Miss Merriman?'

For a second she allowed herself to look into his brilliant, hostile eyes. 'That you're no longer straining to get somewhere. Pushing yourself to the limit.'

'And what would you know about that? Becoming a rich man might be the result of a lot of hard work, but it's even harder to stay there.'

'I suppose so.'

'You must *know* so.' His thick black lashes half veiled his eyes. 'For a girl who was raised like a princess you've built up quite a nice little business,' he drawled.

'Maybe it's because I've still got a lot of rich friends.'

'Even an enemy or two.'

'Are you my enemy, Nick?' she asked.

'No,' he said, with deliberate bluntness. 'It's too long ago.'

'And a lot of things have made you cruel.'

He shifted his hand and skeined a long swathe of her hair around his wrist. 'That's good, coming from you. But the tide has turned completely. Now you're the intruder on my territory.'

'And it makes you happy?'

'Better than that. It's doing wonders for my morale. I can see something else as well. You'll never detach yourself from the old days either. Your father—he turned you into the perennial adolescent. You used to wear your hair like this when you were fourteen years old.'

'In fact,' she said shakily, 'I usually wear it in a coil. I needed hairpins to try and turn that shaft.'

'Oh, I see.' His mouth quirked. 'I daresay you've found another man who likes it long. Vaughn, isn't it? A highly respected profession, the law.'

Dana raised her violet eyes, her lips parted in surprise. 'Who told you that?'

'About your gentleman friend?' There was a sudden flash in his jet black eyes. 'I understand he's proposed several times?'

'Vicki?' she asked.

'I haven't spoken to Vicki in years.' His downbent face was hard and amused. 'No, I keep my little tabs on you, Dana. After all, once we were very close.'

She did not move or reply, and he, too, remained quite still, staring down at her. It was an odd moment, a moment that cut her to the heart and filled him with a kind of inflammatory love-hate.

'Anyway,' he said acidly, 'what's this Vaughn like?'

'A very nice person.'

'Fabulous. What else?'

'He's kind.'

'You like kindness,' he observed.

'I do.'

'You and me both,' he said jeeringly. 'You were very kind to me, Dana.'

'I'm sorry for everything,' she sighed.

'It doesn't matter. It was light years ago.'

From the floor below them, a woman's voice rose.

'Are you up there, Nick?'

'Miss Benson?' Dana looked at him.

He smiled back at her, unpleasantly. 'I gather you didn't take to Jay?'

'Rather, she didn't take to me.'

'Here, Jay,' he called over his shoulder. 'Stay there, we're coming down.'

'I should damned will think so!' Jay Benson cried. 'At this rate, your Mrs Owens will be worn out! She's been racing around everywhere trying to locate that decorator.'

'That's *me*,' Dana whispered as Nick flicked the silky black strand of her hair from his wrist.

He moved closer in a kind of response, an automatic thing that made her ache, then his mouth twisted as if in acknowledgement that he had gone momentarily out of his mind.

'Let's go, Dana,' he said abruptly. 'I don't know why housekeepers love you, but they always do.'

'Where on earth were you?' Jay Benson burst out as soon as they came into sight. Even her hair rose from her face in a kind of frantic resentment.

'Catching up on the old days,' Nick said lightly.

'I was worrying,' she said.

'Stop worrying.' Obviously he still exercised the male prerogative to do exactly as he pleased without much in the way of explanation. 'You two girls know one another, of course.'

'How are you, Miss Benson?' Dana let herself smile.

'I think you owe an apology to Mrs Owens, don't you?'

'She *does*?' Nick faintly emphasised the word.

'Well, she was looking for her, darling,' Jay

Benson explained, moving across to him and slipping an arm around his lean waist. 'It's never easy with you to know exactly what you're getting at.'

'I'll go ahead and find her,' said Dana in her calm, gentle way. 'Actually, I was locked in.'

'And Nick let you out?' Jay Benson's eyes were hard and cold.

'I came a long way to do it specially.'

'Nick!' she rapped on his chest with her knuckles and seeing the excitement in her eyes, Dana turned and moved swiftly along the corridor. Nick and Jay Benson. She didn't have to force herself to accept it. It was inevitable. Men like Nick were a magnet to women and the redhead seemed fairly passionate herself.

It was Nick who insisted Dana stay to lunch, and after it, Dana found her head was aching fiercely. After a few openly patronising remarks which Nick, inexplicably, found indigestible, Jay dropped that pose and pressed Dana with all sorts of interested questions. It was a kind of social sweet-talk which did little to mask the hostility in her narrow dark eyes.

Essentially she disliked Dana and positively distrusted her, as indeed she distrusted all the attractive women that so peppered Nick's life. She even felt impelled to fish for details from Dana's and Nick's past, and in doing so revealed that Nick had never mentioned one word of their old relationship. For that, Dana was profoundly grateful. She had never met a more possessive soul than Jay Benson.

Throughout the delicious, leisurely meal, she had leant constantly towards Nick, touching his hand, his arm, his cheek—simple little gestures a lot more effective than dire warnings. Clearly she was to be regarded as Nick's woman. The first time Dana had met her she had implied that they were only a fortnight away from married life. Which, given Jay's general attitude and Nick's own blatant sexuality, meant all they were short of was a piece of paper. Several times Dana found herself biting back a quick retort, glad a moment later when she encountered the black humour in Nick's eyes. Of course, inevitably the whole story would come out, but Nick should have little difficulty assuring Jay that there was nothing to it. Despite her important position in Nick's life, Jay Benson had obviously decided it was best not to harass him, ridicule the opposition, or resort to the sulks.

At last Dana decided she had just about stood enough. 'I think if you don't mind, I'll run along.'

For the first time Jay gave her a real smile, but Nick merely looked over his glass, raised one black eyebrow and asked: 'Where to?'

'I do have a business.'

'Just so.' He laughed shortly. 'I can't quite grasp what it is you intend to do with the Chinese Room.'

'Chinese Room?' Jay stared at him in astonishment. 'What's Chinese about it?'

Nick's lazy drawl had its attractive, amused note. 'It used to be as Chinese as a Buddhist Kuan Yin.'

'Kuan Yin?' Jay's expression suggested a certain irritation. 'And what exactly's that?'

'A goddess,' Dana explained. 'The Goddess of Mercy and Compassion.'

'Dana knows a lot about that.' Only the faintest trace of acid ate into his voice.

'I see,' Jay frowned at Dana. 'I hope you're not going to turn the place into a museum?'

'I'll turn it into whatever Mr McMasters decides.'

Nick's mouth turned down at the corners, then he smiled. 'Just because I'm your employer, Dana, you don't have to become absurdly formal. Nick will do. Just like the old days.'

It was awkward to say the least with Jay staring sharply from one to the other. 'I thought it might make a nice billiard room,' Jay suggested.

'Billiards? Are you crazy?'

'So many of the people you deal with play billiards, Nick,' Jay told him aggrievedly. 'You know that as well as I do.'

'Just don't expect me to ask them here.' He shrugged and waved his hand at Mrs Owens who was hovering about outside the door waiting to serve them more coffee. 'Mm, lovely,' he smiled at her as she approached him with the coffee pot. 'This is going to be bliss, Mrs Owens, being waited on by you.'

'A pleasure, sir,' Mrs Owens beamed on him indulgently. 'I love to see a man enjoy a good meal.' She placed her plump hand on Dana's shoulder. 'Miss Dana here enjoys my cooking as well, though she hasn't got a single ounce to show for it.'

'Could it be she works too hard?,' Jay Benson said with a glowing look to disguise her ill-will.

'Quite true.' It hadn't occurred to Mrs Owens to mark the contrast between the redhead's words and eyes. 'Many's the time I said to my husband, I'm concerned about that girl.'

'Now, now, Mrs Owens, we're not going to

talk shop!' Dana smiled and held up her coffee cup. Nick had already had his fun with Mrs Owens' enthusiastic openers applauding Dana's 'niceness, conscientiousness and perfect taste'.

'I'll come with you, shall I?' Jay offered later.

'No, you go off and relax,' Nick shrugged negatively.

'I mean it, Nick. I want to come.'

'No, thanks. The best I can do is listen to *one* woman's advice.'

'Pig!'

'That's me,' he agreed blandly. 'Why don't you cool off in the pool?'

'Don't make it long before you join me.' Jay put one hand beneath her fiery mane and shook it out.

Nick nodded carelessly and followed Dana, who had escaped into the quiet hallway. When he looked at her, her expression was serious.

'If you don't like what I've done, Nick, I can change it.'

'Could I ever be disappointed with your perfect taste?'

'It's *your* house.'

Jay passed them, throwing them a tight smile. Today she wore silk pants and a matching halter-necked top in a sophisticated colour combination of chocolate, charcoal and black. She moved well, but Nick didn't follow her progress with his eyes. He was looking around the entrance hall, frowning. When Jay's footsteps had faded away he looked down at Dana, still with that narrow-eyed, formidable expression.

'Aren't you getting a bit too close to the old days?'

'I don't understand, Nick.' She tilted her head

questioningly. Taller than average height, Nick had always made her feel small.

'I don't need a mausoleum to your father.'

Her lips trembled, but she gazed back at him steadily. 'You can't mean that.'

'Maybe *you* don't mean it, but it's the way it's turning out.'

'Then it's simple, isn't it, Nick?' She bowed her head. 'You can dismiss me without a fee.'

'Why dismiss you?' he asked flatly. 'I thought we were old friends. No, Dana, I'm hoping you can normalise it a little.'

'You gave me carte blanche.'

He nodded. 'Maybe I did, and you've made it a vision, but a little too close to Grant Merriman's for my peace of mind.'

'My father had wonderful taste.'

'Terrific,' he interrupted bitterly. 'But now the workers have taken over.'

The hammering inside her head forced her to put two hands to her temples. 'Just tell me what you want changed, Nick.'

'What's wrong with you?' he questioned abruptly.

'I have a headache.'

'So we'll get Mrs Owens to find you some aspirin.'

'*Nick*!' She flung up her head, but her words fell on deaf ears. He was walking away swiftly towards the kitchen.

Dana followed slowly, trying to see what she had done through Nick's eyes. Of course the house, essentially, was much as it had been, but she had introduced many new ideas. It was not possible to break too far from tradition. Or at least Dana was unwilling to. Houses like

Merrilands determined their own interiors and she had put what was left of her heart into her work. As Nick observed—a mausoleum.

He was back within moments, tablets and a glass of water in hand. 'Here you are, dear girl.'

'Can I help it if Mrs Owens like me?'

He didn't answer, but the muscles of his face tightened.

'Maybe I should go home.'

'Why? So you can cry your eyes out?'

Dana shook her head. 'I'm all through with that.'

'Take the tablets, Dana.'

She put them in her mouth, lifted the glass, then swallowed.

'It matters to me we get this thing right.' Nick took the glass out of her nerveless hand and set it down.

'It matters to me, too, Nick. I've spent a good deal of your money.'

'The bronzes.' He ran his fingers consideringly over his cleft chin.

'Ah, *no*, Nick. You know they've been there almost from the beginning.'

'Yeah. They saw *me* getting thrown out of this house.'

'I was distraught at the time,' she pleaded.

'The hell you were! You knew exactly what you were doing—*God damn you!*'

Suddenly Dana was sobbing, and his arm shot out, gathered her in and drew her almost crushingly into the privacy of the study.

'It's like a nightmare!' she moaned, the tears flowing. 'You've been gone years!'

'The making of me.' He gave a harsh laugh.

'Nick, listen. I *can't* work for you.'

'Shut up!'

'Why are you doing this?' she wailed.

'There are worse things I could do.' He brought his two arms around her.

'I'm sure there are,' she said, and her voice was unbearably heartbroken. 'You never used to be a sadist, Nick.'

'Whatever I do I'm trapped.' He said it as though it was wrenched out of him, a painful necessity that had more to do with her slender body close to his than the state of his mind. 'Perhaps if you'd meant less to me, Dana, none of this would be happening. Now I'm finding a certain pleasure in doing this.'

'You must hate me.' She lifted her head, looking up at him with drowning eyes. Her whole being was straining towards him even as her brain was fighting the enormity. One slip now, one offering, and she herself would be in his power. Men loved power, much more than they loved women.

'Oh, I don't hate you, Dana.' There was a faint trembling in his strong arms. 'I'm terrified of you, actually. I don't think that's too exaggerated a word. Surrendering to you was a slide into ecstasy. And hell. When it really came to it, to break from your father, you chose to break me.'

'There was no joy in it, Nick.' She spread her hands against his chest.

'Hating you was all I really wanted to do. I felt the best way to destroy you was to take everything you had. If I'm a millionaire many times over I have you to thank for it, Dana. You and my own ego. You don't even know the kind of hating I'm talking about. Your roots weren't violent. Even when I was developing my first system, it was only a means of making the money to make you suffer. When I sold the rights to the biggest computer company I didn't even care about the money, only the power it could bring me. The fact is, Dana, it was an easy jump from here. It didn't occur to me you would sell.'

'How could I possibly have kept the station going?'

He laughed aloud, crisply. 'A manager, darling. What else?'

'I chose not to.' It didn't matter now to tell him about her father's destructive speculation deals. Grant Merriman had kept up the grandeur right to the end.

'I can't believe it! I thought you would rather sell your soul than Merrilands.'

'It belongs to you now.' Dana said it quietly, standing helpless within the circle of his arms.

'I know. Isn't that ridiculous! Who ever heard of a kid of no importance taking away *your* world?' He smiled, his mouth curving with derision. 'You see, you've brought out the best and the worst in me. Will you marry me?'

Dana couldn't hide the violent shock. 'Knowing your mind, Nick?' She raised an oddly resolute face to him.

'If you're curious about it. You know my body.'

'I won't marry you, Nick. You can have Merrilands, everything else you want, but you'll have to cut short your cruelty there.'

'That's all right, Dana,' he said smoothly, 'I don't want it to be easy.'

She tried to stiffen her body, pull away from him, but he was overwhelmingly stronger. 'Vaughn can't have you, Dana.'

She was overcome by a sudden sweeping anger, a return to the cold fury of yesterday. Ownership, that was all it was. Possession. She thought of her father and Nick. Locked in battle right over her head. She was nothing, only something to be kept, or taken.

'Let me go, Nick,' she said with an icy intensity.

For answer he jerked her harder against him, the bitter smile of understanding on his face. 'Why don't you try throwing me out?'

She tried to tear herself away while he was softly laughing. She twisted her head back and the violent movement hurt her. She wasn't going to plead or cry out. She only hoped Jay Benson would fling herself through the door, then he would have to release her. He had her arms pinned and she could have screamed with her own impotence. The blood was beating all over her, glittering in her veins.

'I hate you, Nick,' she said on a terrible gasping breath, and it was then he pulled her head back and forced his mouth over hers.

It wasn't love or lust but an act of conquest. Dana wanted to deny him access to her open mouth but even in an ecstasy of revulsion her lips parted as though she was starving. Nick was holding her so crushingly it was an additional torture. Perhaps her bones would snap. The thought came to her from the depths of her mind. Please stop. Please stop . . . don't . . . never. . . .

Suddenly it was different, the bruising invasion. The snapping pressure on her body became a cradle and she was losing herself in remembered rapture, trembling violently in Nick's arms. He seemed to whisper something into her open mouth—an involuntary endearment, maybe even a curse. Grief and passion. There was little to choose.

He released her so suddenly she began to sink to her knees and he caught her up again easily, curling his arm around her waist and supporting her until she sank on to the gleaming leather sofa.

'Nothing changes, does it?' he grated.

She ought to put her head down, she was feeling so faint.

His hand clenched lightly on her nape and she fluttered weakly over thinking there was no place on earth to which she could escape.

He was kneeling before her, slapping her wrists. 'You always were unique, Dana,' he said with just the merest remaining trace of tenderness.

It would have been easy to move into his arms, to speak his name, to beg forgiveness, to let him have the freedom of her trembling body, but she knew there were too many dark places dammed up in his soul. He wanted to hurt her. Even when his natural protectiveness surfaced, he couldn't stop.

Very slowly she pulled back from the precipice. 'I'm all right now, Nick.'

He moaned something deep in his throat. 'I'd do anything to have things different, but they're not.'

'No. Revenge. It's one of the oldest, ugliest desires.'

'Of course,' he shrugged it off, then sat down beside her. 'I didn't plan that near-rape.'

'I know that.'

'Sometimes our passions betray even the best of us.'

'At what cost, Nick?' Trembling and spent, she appeared more delicate and beautiful than ever.

'I'm even sorry, but it's necessary.' He smiled at her, no triumph, but implacable determination. She had repulsed him once when he had been frantic with love for her, now when anything was possible for him, he intended to show no mercy.

'Let me out of this contract, Nick.'

'No,' he said quietly, with finality. 'Besides, I like what you've done, I merely propose to change a few things.'

'What?'

He looked at her, noting the pallor of her velvety white skin. 'How can we discuss anything when you're quivering all over? I'll drive you home. We can talk tomorrow. I'm here for a week or until I get a phone call.'

Dana stood up carefully, hoping to goodness Mrs Owens or Jay Benson wouldn't be around to see her. 'You don't have to do that, Nick. I have my car.'

'I saw it,' he said with something like distaste. 'How foolish you are to keep it.'

'I'm afraid my clients expect it.'

'Ah, yes.' He gave her a mocking look of great depth. 'Once a Merriman, always a Merriman. Above all else.'

CHAPTER FIVE

THE news that Nick McMasters was back travelled like wildfire. The whole town, well acquainted with every detail of his past, speculated endlessly on what he really intended to do with the Merriman property. The Staffords had gone. Nick McMasters was the new owner, but it would take a very long time before people could start calling it anything else.

'I think it's downright peculiar,' Keith put forward, his clear skin flushed with heightened colour. 'What would a man who's into robotics want with a sheep station?'

Dana set drinks down on the coffee table before them. 'Maybe he's developing a robot to herd the sheep.'

'It's not funny, Dana,' he stared at her, faintly angry and bewildered. She had only seen McMasters once, yet he suddenly realised to his misery that she had lost a good deal of the remote, Madonna look. Her moulded mouth even looked fuller, as though it had been swollen with violent kisses, and her hair wasn't in its usual immaculate coil but cascading down her back. She looked secretive and exciting. Only one day exposed to McMasters.

'He's planned all this, Dana. You realise that?'

'At least he's put in a first-class manager. Bruce Steele is ideal. He even managed to get Bert to return. I expect Merrilands will concentrate on producing the best clip in the country.'

'I can't imagine what he's thinking of,' Keith persisted. 'I mean, we know what he's all about. Developing software for communication and detection systems is a far cry from collection cups and blue ribbons at the Royal National. I think he did it to spite you—the whole town. I haven't been able to concentrate on a thing since I heard he was back.'

'Have your drink, Keith,' Dana suggested.

'It's bloody awful not knowing what the man's about.' Keith took a deep gulp. 'Why didn't you sack yourself?'

'I signed a contract, Keith, remember?'

'I can get you out of it. I think.'

'I couldn't afford to try.'

'What's he look like?' Keith turned to her urgently.

'Very exotic with that black moustache. Exotic, handsome, a little violent.'

'Bloody-minded, more like it. I hate those raffish, insolent men. How did he treat you?'

'I think I'll have to change quite a lot of things,' Dana said worriedly.

'*What!*' Keith's smooth skin flushed scarlet. 'You mean to tell me a boor like McMasters has questioned your taste?'

'Perhaps he can see something I can't,' Dana murmured.

'Rubbish! You know he's only trying to humiliate you. He's going to treat you like a servant. Worse than you people treated his mother.'

'Oh, Keith!' Dana gasped, and leaned back as if she had received a blow over the heart. 'Mrs McMasters was always treated well. My God, there was no way else to treat her. She was so small and fragile, so softly spoken.'

'You told me all about that incident with a dress. Don't you remember? The way McMasters turned it into a pretty grim confrontation. You might have been wandering around in your fantasy world, Dana, but it must have been vile for him—only allowed in the back door, his mother ironing and mending. Why did you choose such a sorry little soul to work for you?'

'She needed work, Keith. She really needed work to earn money. And I've given you the wrong impression. She wasn't a sorry little soul, she was a very brave lady. She had to cope with tragedy—the loss of her husband and child and keeping on going with never a sign of her terrible pain. She lived for Nick. As long as her frail body held out, but I've never met a woman I've admired more.'

'How touching!'

'It needn't concern you.' Dana spoke coldly and it brought Keith up short.

'Don't be emotional, darling.'

'You're the one who's being emotional, Keith,' she pointed out.

'I'm sorry, but what else can you expect? I love you, Dana. I want and need you desperately, and all the time I have this terrible fear you'll go running back to McMasters.'

'It's much too late for that,' Dana assured.

He leaned forward so he could see more than her pure profile. 'You mean that woman he has with him? It's serious?'

'I mean Nick and I belong to the past tense. It's absolutely over.'

'Oh, Dana, If I could believe that!' He drew her towards him and nuzzled his face into her neck. She was so lovely yet austere, like a goddess. 'Suppose we were to get engaged?'

Dana knew at once it was a solution. Perfect, except for one thing. She didn't love Keith. Her heart had been chained irrevocably.

'Darling!' A wave of desire broke over Keith's head and his hands ached to touch her, caress her breasts. He moved closer, emboldened, because her head was tilted back and her violet eyes half closed. 'Why don't you let me make love to you? *Why?*'

She seemed to be oblivious to him, so he slipped his hand beneath the fold of her beautiful embroidered robe, seeking her white breasts. He had never seen skin like hers; the texture and the luminosity. 'You're so beautiful,' he breathed.

Still she didn't move and he pushed the robe aside. Her breasts were as tender as a young girl's, the nipples soft pink. Now her eyes were tightly closed and a flush shadowed the high, delicate cheekbones.

'The first time you've let me do that,' he whispered shakily. 'I want you so much, Dana. Let me take you into the bedroom?'

He went to raise her up, but suddenly she came to life. 'Oh——' A tremor shook her trance-like body.

'You're the worst kind of tease, Dana,' he told her.

'I'm sorry.' She touched his arm placatingly.

'Perhaps you were fantasising that it was McMasters? He knows all about your body, doesn't he?'

Dana turned away from him, her long hair falling over her shoulder. With her white skin, long jet-black hair and the gorgeous silk kimono draped around her she might have been some beautiful geisha trained to give pleasure.

'Why did I have to choose you?' Keith asked bitterly. 'Why *you*? You're impossible!'

'And you're unfair and you know it!' A quick turn of her head and the submissive look was slashed. There was too much hauteur in the face, too much spirit. Her large eyes were violet, not meekly lowered, but staring him down. 'You've been trying to push me into bed from the second time we were together.'

'Gentlemen don't attempt it the first time.' Her sudden fierceness, as usual, had him backing down.

Sighing, she gazed at him, the fire spent. 'I don't love you, Keith. I'm very, very sorry.'

'You're twenty-six, Dana,' he said. 'Soon you'll be thirty. I'm offering you marriage, the chance for a family—a small one. What you're suffering from is a long-seated hang-up. McMasters did that to you, the miserable bastard!'

Keith was right.

The next morning Dana didn't go to Merrilands as arranged, but straight to the shop. The phone rang just as she let herself in the door.

'Keith, darling! I just wanted to say I'm sorry about last night.'

She heard him out with a kind of melancholy attention, and less than twenty minutes later two dozen perfect pink roses were delivered to the door.

Jenny took them without much enthusiasm. 'They're from Mr Vaughn.'

'How do you know?'

'They look kinda prim. Anyway, I can see the card.'

'You're not supposed to read it, Jenny,' Dana said firmly.

'I didn't really. I just saw—Keith.'

The phone rang again and Dana, very much on edge, jumped. It was only one of her clients making enquiries about when her sofas, at the upholsterers, were coming back, and of course, just before she hung up she asked about Nick . . . 'Didn't we always say he'd have a very bright future!'

Dana remembered exactly what Mrs Winterman had said. Just as she expected Mrs Winterman was going to put it firmly out of her mind. It was one of the oldest ironies in the world. When you were down you were dead, but when you were on top old enemies turned into simpering admirers.

'Where do you want me to put these roses?' Jenny asked.

'They're lovely!' As if for consolation Dana gently stroked a petal. 'No room on my desk. Put them on the table over there.'

Jenny's big eyes were brilliant with curiosity. 'How did it go yesterday?' she asked.

'Not altogether successfully.'

'You mean to say he didn't like it?' Jenny screeched.

Dana went to answer her, then froze with dismay. A red Jaguar slid to a halt right outside and as she shrank back defensively Nick's tall, rangy body hove into sight. Even from a distance his eyes were like burning coals.

'Oh, my!' Jenny gasped. She had never seen such an electrifying man in her life.

'Good morning.' Nick had pushed the door

open, giving Jenny the same lazy smile that galvanised young girls and old ladies alike.

'Good morning, Mr McMasters,' Jenny twinkled coquettishly, and Nick gave her another glance.

'Aren't you the little Stevens girl?'

'Fancy you remembering!' Jenny was now positively sparkling.

'You look charming, *Jenny*.'

'Heck, you must have perfect recall!'

'It *can* work against you,' Nick said. 'Are you still with your grandmother?'

'Oh, yes! She's still quite hale.'

'Say hello to her for me.'

'Oh, sure!' Jenny looked at him star-struck. 'We both saw you on television.'

Dana's slender body seemed to rise of its own will. Her mind wasn't functioning properly at all. It was Jenny who was displaying the panache, no doubt playing up to Nick's swashbuckling image.

Gradually he noticed her. 'Hi, Dana.' The curves of his mouth deepened sardonically. 'I like your idea of an early morning start.'

Though she felt contempt for herself she began to apologise. 'I was going to ring you, Nick. There were certain things I had to do here.'

'Like wait for her flowers,' Jenny said.

'Flowers?' He swung around and laughed. Jenny had just crammed the roses into a crystal vase. 'Precisely what I'd expect Vaughn to send to you.'

'I love them,' said Dana.

'They'll last a lot longer if you space them out.'

Jenny looked at him, experiencing the first real lurch of excitement in her young life. 'It just struck me then that I should have used another vase.'

'Why don't you, young Jenny?'

'The blue and white one, Jenny,' Dana suggested, as Jenny seemed rooted to the spot.

'Nice little kid. A cheeky cherub,' Nick remarked lightly as they were driving away.

'She fell in love with you on sight.'

'She was supposed to.' He glanced at her sidelong and laughed. Today he looked quite different, she saw with astonishment. Gone the smouldering ruthlessness and in its place an easy tolerance that was equally turbulent. He was devastatingly good-looking, the more so in maturity.

'You weren't coming, were you?' he said.

'No.' Out of the shop and away from Jenny she saw no reason to deny it.

'You've got to go through with it, Dana. Otherwise I'll get mad.'

'Is Miss Benson there this morning?' she asked.

He nodded. 'Does it hurt?'

'How can you use her like that, Nick?'

'I'm selfish—plain selfish. Jay knows the score.'

'She loves you,' Dana sighed.

'Women like Jay don't understand love. They go in and out of affairs.'

'So do you.'

'In a big way,' he agreed.

'And I expect they would continue even if I was crazy enough to put myself in your power?'

'I guess so. I no longer believe in fidelity.'

'Your own, you mean? I'm certain that wouldn't apply to your wife.'

'You know me so well, Dana.' His eyes flickered over her for a few seconds. 'They tell me you can't seem to take this Vaughn seriously?'

'Who tells you, Nick?'

'That's what makes it delicious. It's a secret. I must look up this guy. Hell, it's possible I could put a little work his way.'

'The thing is,' Dana said, 'he knows about you.'

'*Me?*'

'Us,' she corrected.

'You mean you told him I was your lover?'

Her blue-violet eyes gazed sightlessly out the window. 'He knew without my telling him,' she lied.

'So you're sleeping with him,' Nick said harshly.

She glanced at him and saw the tell-tale muscle jerking beside his mouth.

Silence.

Dana swallowed on a very real anger. The freedom that was part and parcel of being male, the strict behaviour demanded of a woman even if that strictness was a protection for their greater vulnerability.

Nick drove the car off the road, switched off the ignition and turned on her. His earlier expression had only been camouflage, now he looked as profoundly dangerous as a black panther. 'Well? I asked you just now were you sleeping with him?'

'What do you think I get by on? Dreams?' she spoke wildly, anger intertwined with the desire to hurt, and he lifted his hand as though he was going to strike her.

'Go on, hit me.'

Nick shook his head, as much to clear it as in rejection.

'I remember what you're like when you freak out.' Now the tears were threatening as intense emotions sprang into play. 'You look strange, Nick, for a man who's shaken me off. If I didn't know differently I'd think you were suffering.'

She wasn't aware of how he did it, but somehow they were struggling outside the car. She felt odd now, sick and weak. 'I haven't slept with him, Nick,' she moaned. 'There was never any question of it.'

'And neither will you.' He was shaking her so furiously she was nearly launched into the air. 'Early relationships can blight one's whole life. They go too deep to brook interference. You belong to me.'

'I don't *want* to belong to you, Nick,' she cried in a kind of terror. 'You're too primitive!'

'Wow!' he muttered.

There was no chance she could struggle free. When Nick was in a certain mood he could be likened to the devil himself.

What brought them both to their senses was the sound of an approaching car.

'I think, *truly*, one day I'll strangle you,' Nick told her. 'You never let up until I'm half crazy.'

Oh, there was truth in it, Dana thought shakily. Once he had accused her of provoking him until he turned into a madman.

'It was a mistake, Nick, to come back,' she said.

'Get into the car!' He gripped her shoulder, his fingers biting into the soft skin.

The approaching vehicle came closer, stopped on the other side of the road. Until this moment neither had been really aware of it, except as a heavensent interruption, but now Dana looked in amazement as Vicki danced across the road to greet them.

'Nick! Good old Nick!' She threw out her arms and gave him a cheerful, excited smile.

'My God, the proud little mother!' He gathered her into a bear hug, then when she lifted her head, kissed her mouth.

'You're gorgeous. *Gorgeous!*' she cried.

'*Numero uno,*' he laughed.

'Dana, darling, isn't he something!' Vicki now hugged Dana to her. 'I rang to tell you I was coming over, but Jenny told me you'd driven off.'

'And where's your son and heir?' Nick glanced back towards Jenny's dusty station wagon.

'He's with Mum. Don't worry, you'll see him. And Dave. None of us can seem to adjust to this great news. Our Nick a millionaire, a computer genius. As different from most people——'

'As he always was.'

Vicki gave a stage cough. 'Now what were you two talking about?'

'Certainly not old times.' Nick put his arm around Vicki with the careless ease of an old friend. 'Are you going to follow us up to the house?'

'Try and stop me!' Vicki looked around for Dana. 'Am I allowed to see what you've done?'

'My dear,' Nick drawled, 'you're going to be dazzled!'

To begin with they were met by Jay Benson in a white lycra bikini against which her skin glowed a rich bronze.

'S'truth!' Vicki hissed in Dana's ear. 'Who's that?'

Dana looked at her friend quite collectedly.

'That's Nick's paramour, mistress, lover, old lady, duck, broad, chick. . . .'

'Lucky devil—and half naked to boot! If I were you, girl, I'd cut my hair and get in there,' Vicki advised.

'Cut my hair?' Dana echoed.

'Like you used to.' Vicki screwed up her eyes. 'God, she's thin! Really she's not exactly Nick's type. Even at your slimmest you've always had a lovely little bosom.'

'Oh, *Vicki!*' Dana felt herself sliding again towards mad laughter.

Jay Benson looked at them both as though they were pathetic. Chasing after Nick. This morning, apart from the minuscule bikini she was wearing a heavy, distinctive perfume, and was rewarded when Nick kissed her twice on the neck.

'I don't think he wants her at all,' Vicki whistled through her teeth. 'He's just trying to pay you back.'

'For what?'

'Dearest——' Vicki leaned towards her, 'you did a lot of damage, I understand. You had your father to consider, but breaking off your engagement had a vast effect on Nick. Why don't you marry him and make it up to him?'

'That, too, would be a frightful mistake.'

If it was possible for people to wring their hands, Vicki wrung hers. The tangle Nick and Dana had got themselves into was enough to make anyone weep.

But the house was lovely! Vicki walked around exclaiming. 'And when, Nick, are you going to actually move in?'

'I won't be living here, Vicki, but I plan on being here a lot. I could use it for conferences, as far as that goes. Entertaining my overseas guests. A lot of them like to see the "real Australia", so they tell me.'

'Kangaroos and koalas?'

'Something like that.'

Jay had now joined them, a diaphanous garment veiling her white bikini, and Nick put out his arm to her. 'Jay has often acted as my hostess.'

'I bet your guests spend their time following *her* around!' Vicki chuckled.

'Do you blame them?'

'Not one bit.'

It was all too friendly for words, and now that Jay had learned Vicki had a husband and a two-year-old son, she was encouraged to be pleasant. To Vicki. It concluded with Jay and Vicki taking tea beside the pool while Nick, all trace of geniality worn off, snapped off the changes he wanted made. Nothing major. It was more a matter of assembling things differently and simply taking some things out.

'I'm not after the perfect room, Dana,' he told her.

'Neither am I.' She had worked out the placing of the furniture quite logically—a process that left the drawing room looking almost exactly as it was. 'These were only provisional arrangements anyway. In fact I've never worked without my client. You gave me a free rein, now you're lecturing me on what I've done wrongly.'

'Not wrongly, Dana—the same. You can't get very far from your memories.'

'Tradition,' she said heatedly. 'Don't probe and analyse *me*, Nick. You're too complicated yourself.'

In the end it was decided to turn the Chinese Room into the equivalent of a boardroom but without the usual boardroom austerity. Now that he was here, he was as definite in his ideas as a lot of her clients were uncertain.

'And by the way, I want a piano in the drawing room—a Steinway. You can arrange it.'

'Miss Benson plays?' Dana queried.

'*Games*,' he mocked her. 'She likes lots of fun.'

'And none too proper.'

'She's not half so passionate as you. There, that tears you, doesn't it, darling? Behind the Madonna face a powerful sexuality.'

'You monster, Nick!' she muttered.

'Let me cover my ears. You're judging poor old Jay far too harashly. *You're* the one who can lash up a storm.'

She actually bit her tongue to prevent a retort, then walked shakily away to the door. 'Do you want me to submit plans for this room, Nick?' she asked.

'No, go ahead.'

'Oh, I thought you didn't like what I've done, one little bit.'

'Darling, I love it, as you know very well. I just don't want to look at exactly the same view.'

'That's ridiculous.' Her face couldn't quite control her hurt. 'Everything is really quite different—and, I hope, forward-looking.'

'I know that.' He came to stand beside her so she had to keep her head tilted. 'It's just that it's not immediately apparent. Emotions are messy and I can't look at this house painlessly.'

'Or me.'

'I'm glad you accept it.'

She didn't realise she was staring into his eyes as a woman only looks at her lover.

'For God's sake——'

'What *is* it?' Something in the quality of his expression frightened her.

Nick turned his head away, his bold face saturnine. 'Nothing. I just thought you were trying a few little tricks out for size.'

'Tricks?' Her violet eyes went cloudy. 'Tricks haven't entered my head. Shall you pick the piano out, Nick, or shall I?'

'I don't know a thing about pianos, Dana,' he murmured. 'You're the one with all the accomplishments.'

'I couldn't get a Steinway here.'

'Then fly back with me when I go.'

It was flung at her carelessly, but he knew the moment he had said it that light aircraft were now indissolubly linked with her father's tragedy. Her lovely skin blanched and her inner disturbance showed up in her eyes.

'Dana?' His long stride had him instantly at her side.

'I could never do that, Nick.'

'You can't afford not to.' His hands dropped to her shoulders, not gripping, but exquisitely gentle. 'Flying is our way of life. Think of the time Duchess shied and threw you. You took a bad toss, but you just started up again.'

'This is different, Nick. Besides, I can manage my own affairs.'

He looked carefully into her white face. 'I want you to come with me when I go. There's no need to be fearful. You used to love flying.'

'Not any more.' With his black eyes intent on her, her anxiety increased. Nick had always pushed her to the limit. 'I can drive in or take a domestic flight. I'd feel a whole lot safer in a jet.'

'I *want* you to come with me.'

She shook her head. 'I'm sure Miss Benson would be delighted to see me go to pieces.'

He looked down at her sharply. 'Jay is taking the car back. The whole of life is facing up to things—painful things. Anyway,' his glance became mocking, 'I'm a magnificent pilot.'

'I think you'd be a magnificent anything, Nick,' she burst out almost wrathfully.

'Thank you very much, darling. If you look like playing up on me, I'll get you a little drunk.' He suddenly touched her cheek, communicating such tenderness, sensitivity, power, she thought she would dissolve at his feet.

'*Don't*, Nick.' She was aching with the effort not to fall forward into his arms.

'Why? Does it hurt?' He sounded desperately casual. He drew her into his arms and suddenly brought his hands up beneath her breasts. 'You know I want you. I don't understand why I want you—the whole thing's beyond me.'

Her whole body trembled with desire. What she wanted . . . Oh God, it was impossible . . . impossible. . . .

'My poor Dana! Our karma is really one another, whether we want it or not.' He was looking down at her gravely, for once without the furious, single-minded hostility that made him behave violently.

'It frightens me,' she said. Now his hands were cupping her breasts and she knew she was clinging to him blindly. It took only seconds for ecstasy to flower and she saw his face harden into a sensual mask.

'I want to make love to you. *Now*,' he said urgently.

'Of course you do!' Realisation of her own weakness made the words come out in a little scorching hiss. 'So many women just waiting around for you to make love to them. Do we tell Jay or not?'

'Ridiculous, darling. I never tell.'

Her head was still swimming from the effect of those caressing fingers, but she jerked herself away. 'You might be out to destroy my self-respect, but I intend to preserve it.'

'Do you think it would be a good thing?' he taunted her. 'You're twenty-six. One can't pretend you're getting any younger.'

There was a cushion lying on an armchair and though Dana never cared for wild behaviour she could not go on like this. She picked it up and hurled it, and Nick fielded it just like a basketball player.

'Such second-rate behaviour from *you*, Miss Dana, simply will not do!'

The words and the tone were reproduced with the utmost accuracy. Mrs Cameron, their old housekeeper and Nick's enemy, had often cautioned her in just that way when she had been a little girl.

She could never protect herself from Nick. She gave a funny, desolate little cry, aware that he was staring at her with eyes beyond comfort, then she turned and fled through the house to the rear garden where Vicki was becoming more and more bored with Jay Benson's conversation.

As soon as she saw Dana, she seized the opportunity to jump up. 'Decided on what you're going to do?'

Jay Benson, stretched out in a recliner, opened her eyes. 'You took an awfully long time,' she drawled.

'Sorry. It's not easy to arrive at a compromise sometimes.'

'O.K., sweetie?' Vicki caught Dana's hand, surprised and concerned at her pallor.

'I'd love a cup of tea—coffee. Anything.'

'I'm sure Mrs Owens will be delighted to get you one,' Jay drawled. 'I don't know anything about housekeepers myself. We never had the money to lead a useless life.'

'Why, how unfair of you, Miss Benson,' Vicki said with a sharp smile. 'Dana lost her mother when she was only a little girl. A housekeeper, so to speak, was a necessity.'

'Oh, go on with you, though it's refreshing to see you so loyal to your friend. The rich invariably have them. Doesn't Miss Merriman look a rich girl? Even now that she's not. There's a very real difference, you know, between the born rich and those that make it to the top. Take Nick, for instance. His early life must have been pretty awful, though I dare not ask him about it. But it shows. He's a very complex man. He has no illusions. He never speaks of love. Women go mad just looking at him, but he hasn't a romantic bone in his body. Passion, yes, more than you could possibly handle, but he does *not* fall in love. In fact he prides himself he doesn't need any one of us. The truth of it nearly put one of our glamorous society gals into a mental hospital. Me, I cry no tears,' Jay added.

'Do you love him?' Dana asked, with a serious, compassionate expression.

'Sure I do, but not quite in the sense you

mean. Nick has always been honest with me. He gives me money and a good time. I *have* to be satisfied, and so is he. If it came to it and he really did marry someone, I might jump in the harbour. No, I mightn't. I've a feeling Nick will marry some perfect, luxurious creature like Miss Merriman here.' The words were savage. 'It will help him forget about his childhood. He exhibits all the classic symptoms of the self-made man. He wants a fantastic old heap like this and a woman of impeccable background. He doesn't have to love her. Nick's unscrupulous about getting what he wants.'

'No one can say that of him in business,' Vicki said sharply. 'He's become a highly respected and distinguished man.'

'And a big contributor to worthy charities,' Jay laughed cynically. 'Nick knows what he's doing. None better. I expect they'll knight him at about forty. You've got to hand it to the boy— from a penniless, fatherless brat, to one of the brightest boys in the country. A powerful man with the government devoted to him. Some kind of brain! They contact him from all over the world to correct their little problems. Do you know, he even had to go to the States to work on some missile control system. So they haven't got all the brains there.'

'He always was brilliant,' Vicki offered as Dana remained silent. 'I remember him helping one of the teachers at high school with *his* own university assignment. Things came to him so naturally it makes one wonder about re-incarnation. His father was only a crop-duster and his mother was just an ordinary little woman.'

'She wasn't ordinary at all,' Dana said with some difficulty. 'She was an exquisite needle-woman, and I can remember her talking to me sometimes. She wasn't a simple, ordinary woman at all. Life just forced her into a very ordinary situation.'

'Now you thoroughly surprise me, Miss Merriman,' Jay exclaimed. 'Your friend sounds the snob and you sound most reasonable. Is there no end to surprises?'

'You misunderstand me,' Vicki protested.

'No, I don't.' Jay glanced down at her long, racehorse legs unperturbed. 'Truly egalitarian people are very much in a minority, and I suspect they come from the privileged classes.'

Mrs Owens was now hurrying across the lawn. 'Ah, there you are, Miss Dana.' She came to a halt beside Dana, looking down at her with real affection. 'You look pale, dear. Are you all right?'

'I'd love a cup of tea, Mrs Owens.' Dana looked up urgently.

'Then you shall have one, and a couple of my cup cakes as well.'

'Privileged classes!' said Jay.

CHAPTER SIX

IT was fascinating to watch Mario work on the restoration of the coffered ceiling. Dana found herself popping in to see him when she should have been doing something else.

'You're doing a beautiful job, Mario,' she called to him. 'I don't know whatever I would have done without you.' Which was perfectly true, as craftsmen of the order of Mario were extremely rare indeed.

'You want I should look at the ceiling in the gallery?'

'No, don't bother now. Some time today when you come down the ladder.'

Mario smiled in his gentle way. 'Just as you like. I was going to suggest one or two things.'

'Whatever you think, Mario. You're so clever.'

'Tell me more!' the elderly man laughed, and went to turn back to the job but as Dana gazed in horror the ladder began to slide.

'Mario—help!' She rushed to hold it, and startled and alarmed, Mario jumped.

'Let me help you, *signorina*.' He managed to do something, but the ladder fell with a sickening weight against Dana's shoulder and as she cried out hollowly eventually brought her down.

Mario was now wailing loudly in Italian while Dana lay on her side with odd little lights flickering in front of her vision. She wondered if she had broken something, but she didn't think so. Winded, more likely. She felt very strange.

'*Mamma mia, mamma mia*, what am I to do?' Mario was down on his knees beside her. 'Please, *please*, Miss Dana, don't be hurt!'

She tried to speak to him, but she couldn't find the breath.

'I must go to get help.' He jumped up in agitation, his swarthy skin pallid.

'My God, what's the matter?' Nick was there suddenly, the easy, interested expression shocked from his face. He had expected to see Mario at work on the ceiling yet here he was hunched over Dana, twisting his hands in the most abject misery. 'Dana?' Nick fell to his knees, his own golden skin blanching.

'*Please!*' That hoarse little voice couldn't be her own.

'Of course it is my fault!' Mario announced on a rush of agony. 'Always, always, I take care with the ladders, but today I must have been careless. This poor little girl broke my fall.'

'Perhaps you could get Mrs Owens to ring the doctor,' Nick told him. 'Then I want you to have a brandy. You'll find some in the study.'

'No, no, I'm fine. It is this child here.'

'Get help,' Nick ordered.

'Certainly. At once.' Mario grasped Dana's hand, then rushed off.

'Are you in pain, Dana?' Nick asked her. 'Show me.'

She turned over gingerly, lying on her back. Gradually she was regaining her breath. 'Poor old Mario! Go and calm him. He could have a heart attack.'

'Janet will settle him.' His hands began to move gently from her collarbone over her shoulders and down her arms.

'I'll probably be black and blue.'

'How the hell did it happen?' he puzzled.

'How do any accidents happen?'

'Carelessness. One can't be allowed to drift into it.'

'Oh, Mr McMasters!' Mrs Owens rushed in.

'Did you ring the doctor, Janet?'

'He's coming right away.'

'I don't need him—I'm fine,' protested Dana.

'Fine, are yah?' Even Mrs Owens had lost her ruddy glow. 'It's a remarkable piece of luck if you are! I said to Mario myself, that's a parquet floor.'

'Oh, don't scold him. He's in such a state.'

'She hasn't broken anything, has she?' Mrs Owens asked worriedly. 'What an idiotic thing!'

'No, I don't really think so.' Nick was still observing Dana's colour. 'When she feels a little better I'll take her upstairs.'

'I'm *all right*.' Dana went to sit up, winced and lay back.

'I've been praying!' Mario reappeared, nursing an empty crystal tumbler. 'Oh, lord, what can I say?'

'Have another brandy, Mario,' Nick said.

'If I start, I mightn't stop.' Seeing Dana's colour returning, Mario began to breathe easier. 'So brave! She should really have let me fall.'

'That's the usual thing with ladders.' Nick put his arms beneath Dana and lifted her. 'All right?'

'In any case, would you listen?' she muttered.

'No.'

They formed a little procession up the stairs until they arrived at the door of the master bedroom. Mario was still chattering away to himself in Latin and Nick glanced rather wryly at his housekeeper. 'I don't think one drink was sufficient, Janet, and this isn't exactly a social scene.'

'Good heavens, no.' Mrs Owens looked purposeful and kindly. She placed one stout hand on Mario's arm and obediently moved him off. 'No need to go fussin' the Almighty, Mario,' she said, 'it's not so terrible after all. Miss Dana hasn't broken anything.'

'Oh, God is so good!'

'I can't possibly lie there!' Dana protested horrified by erotic images of Jay Benson and Nick.

'Banish your lascivious thoughts. Jay and I have had a purely platonic relationship this week,' Nick assured her.

'*Liar!*'

'No, darling, it's the anguished truth. Anyway, Jay has the Oriental woman's angle on fleshly pleasures. Her master's needs or lack of them are all that seem important.'

'How absolutely dreadful!' She seemed to sink deeply into the huge bed. It was far from new to her, apart from the modern ensemble that mercifully slid into place within its magnificent antique mahogany surrounds. The whole suite was so huge, for all its grandness it had been refused at auction. So at Merrilands for which it had been made in Victorian England, it remained.

'Can you get that blouse off?' Nick asked her.

'I will when the doctor comes.'

'*Ah!*' He sat down beside her and raised his quirky brows. 'It just so happens to be important to me. *Now*.'

'I'm sure I believe that.'

'Show me, darling—please! I am capable of the clinical approach, you know.'

'You see?' She arched her back a little. 'I can't get up.'

'Then I'll just have to undress you as though you were a child. I seem to recall helping you a lot with bathing suits and pinafores and whatever.'

There was a silence between them that brought tears to her eyes. 'No one could have been kinder to me, Nick, than you were. No, don't smile like that—just like a tiger. I loved you, I worshipped you. You were the big brother I never had. My father would have adored to have you as his son. You didn't know that, did you? *He* knew it in his heart.'

'Ah, yes—a son. Never a lover for his daughter. As soon as I became that, I encountered hatred. The Greeks used to write plays about that sort of thing.' He leaned towards her and she put out her hand uncertainly. 'Sit up, Dana. I'll help you.'

'I know perfectly well what you'll do.' Although he had known every inch of her body she was blushing and trembling in a kind of alarm.

'There now.' He had her sitting up. 'I'm afraid you've torn your blouse. I'll get you another.'

'I'm not prepared to let you.'

'*God*, darling!' He was staring at the bruising that was already apparent on her white shoulder.

'Oh, heavens!' Dana found herself exclaiming at the marred perfection.

He had her blouse completely off her and it slid unnoticed to the floor. Because it was sheer she wore a tiny, matching shell-pink camisole over her bra, dipping in a deep V between her breasts.

'Oh, that looks ugly, doesn't it?' She suddenly felt sick.

'Ugly?' He put his mouth on her shoulder.

'Nick!' Her eyes widened and she looked towards the open door.

'Never mind. We could hear someone coming a mile off. Who's to come anyway. Jay's in town and Mrs Owens knows the score.'

'Score?' Dana queried.

'Never you mind.'

Now her heart was racing out of control.

'You're afraid of me?' he asked gently.

Her nipples, ever sensitive, peaked in urgent arousal, and her violet eyes glowed and glittered in a face that was no longer white but flushed with hot blood.

He eased her back on to the pillows, then bent over her, his mouth moving slowly across her shoulder, over the curve of her breast into the scented cleft. They might have been cut off from the rest of the world.

'This is agony,' he muttered.

Despite herself her hands found his head, her fingers spearing in to the thick hair that would curl if he let it.

'Yes,' she said unevenly. 'Frightful to have no pride.'

'Maybe pride is a waste of time.'

She sighed, lost in sensation and sadness. Had she and Nick been quite alone, far from interruption, denial would have been more than she could humanly stand. Only the knowledge that someone, even now, could surprise them guaranteed control.

'No woman's skin is like yours. It doesn't look the same, or feel the same, or have this delicate, elusive scent.' He traced a finger down a fragile blue vein.

'Please, Nick, someone might come.' Her voice was slipping away on her.

'*This* time.' His eyes touched along her body. 'For just short periods it's still possible to believe nothing bad ever happened between us. I'm deliriously young. We're together. I suppose it really did scare me, and it should have. Maybe it's like they say. The cat can't look at the Queen. A beggar can't hunger after the princess.'

'Nick, you'll make me cry!' she whispered.

'I thought that's what I wanted.' He looked down into her still face, his expression faintly brutal. 'Did your father really have his heart attack?'

She visibly shrank back.

'*Did* he?' He put a little pressure beneath her chin.

'Of course.' She had an intense desire to protect her father.

'The perfect daughter! Even now.' He stood up and moved to the French doors that led out on to the wrought-iron enclosed verandah. 'Solid old Dr Anderson is coming. After all this time and he still drives the same car.'

'Uncle Arthur.'

'Yes, dear old Uncle Arthur. Let's see, he's in love with you as well.'

'He always championed you,' she pointed out.

'The hell he did!' Nick's strong, definite features had hardened. 'He might have said a few kind words once in a while, but he was always your father's stooge. If Grant Merriman told him to say something, he'd say it. Good old helpful Arthur. For payment your father built a new hospital wing.'

A short time later, Arthur Anderson was standing beside the bed. 'No need for any X-rays, I'm certain there's nothing broken.'

Nick nodded rather mockingly. 'We had to be sure.'

'Sister gave the message to Dr Barker, but I decided to come.'

'That's a consolation to Dana.'

'Thank you, Uncle Arthur,' Dana looked up into the familiar, kindly grey eyes. 'Now that you've given me the all clear, I'm going to get up.'

'You'll be pretty stiff and sore for a day or two. I'll give you a liniment to rub in—and have you an infra-red ray lamp?'

'No.' Dana's voice sounded a little feathery and weak.

'We can easily get one,' said Nick.

'Your housekeeper might have one,' Dr Anderson suggested. 'So many people do in case of aches and pains. Here, let me help you, Dana.' He helped her gravely back into her blouse. 'No rush to get back on the job in the morning, is there, Nick?'

'Of course not. Dana knows that.'

'Destiny, eh?' the doctor muttered, looking from one to the other. 'Welcome back, Nick.'

Towards the end of the week, as Dana was showing a prospective client out of the showroom, the red Jaguar came to rest in the only remaining parking spot. A moment later Jay Benson stood out and Dana waited for her politely at the door.

'Shall we go in?'

'Certainly. Do you wish to speak to me?'

The redhead nodded. 'Very much.'

Jenny, who was unwrapping beautiful little boxes for coffee tables, looked up expectantly.

'Get lost, kid,' ordered Jay.

'Shall I?' Jenny looked at Dana for direction.

'Well——' Dana looked at Jay Benson's tormented face, 'take an early lunch.'

'No money.' Jenny turned the pockets of her pink dress out. 'I bought a pair of shoes and it bit deep into the old budget.'

'Here.' Dana took five dollars out of her handbag and put it into Jenny's hand. 'While you're gone, you can call in to Markwell Brothers and see what's happened to Mrs Winterman's sofas. I've never known them to be so slow.'

'I know why,' said Jenny with a strong look of her grandmother. 'Harry Markwell's wife has left him. Went off with one of the salesmen they deal with.'

'Callous bitch!' Jay Benson laughed. 'Beat it, kid.'

Spoken to so nicely, Jenny retreated in a hurry.

'Please sit down, Miss Benson,' Dana said mildly.

'Thanks. You haven't got a drink, have you?'

'What would you like?'

'Not water, that's for sure.'

Dana hesitated, not even sure what she meant. Did one feel like spirits at eleven o'clock in the morning? Fleetingly she observed Jay Benson again. One did.

Jay received her drink with a curt nod of thanks. 'How are you, anyway? How's the shoulder?'

'A lovely shade of purple with blue and green streaks.'

'You were lucky. You could have broken your collarbone.'

'Mario broke the weight,' Dana explained.

'So you were engaged to Nick?' Jay Benson burst out baldly.

'Yes.'

'You might have told me.'

'It was years ago—in the past.'

'I got talking to someone in the town. The woman from that rather surprising little boutique.'

'Sonia Eden?'

'Sonia Something, yes. She was a veritable mine.'

'I'm surprised Nick never told you,' said Dana.

'My dear, Nick tells me nothing—absolutely nothing. Women aren't at all important to Nick. Or so I thought. He has a great capacity for driving them crazy while remaining very detached himself. That Sonia woman, however, suggested that he had some kind of a sublime relationship with you.'

'Why would she bring up an old story?' Dana asked quietly.

'Maybe I urged her on.' This morning, unaccountably, Jay looked much older. 'Of course I knew you were a phoney.'

'Really?'

Jay Benson spoke dully. 'I'm not usually afraid of Nick's other women, even the high society chicks like Janette Holman, but I was afraid of you.'

'But why?'

'You know how it is—*instinct*. It's not that I dislike you. I could like you very much, except I have the terrible feeling Nick wants you.'

Dana's blue-violet eyes were wide and distant. 'You're using the wrong tense,' she said.

The other woman laughed aloud. 'You know damned well I'm not. The other day when you hurt yourself he couldn't even keep his feelings buttoned up. Our inscrutable Nick! It was a big shock for me, and I've known him for years.'

'I'm sorry, but it makes no difference. What Nick and I shared is in the past. It's not possible to reform that same relationship again.'

'Is it necessary to have the same relationship?' Jay Benson asked with a twisted smile.

'Anything else would only cause more suffering.'

Jay Benson rose and set down her empty glass. 'I can see you don't want to talk.'

'There's nothing to talk about.' Dana's dark hair gleamed with purple lights.

'I can't attempt to understand you at all,' Jay sighed. 'You could have Nick if you wanted him.'

Dana lifted her eyes to the other woman and smiled strangely. 'At what price?'

Jenny arrived back an hour later. 'Has she gone?'

'She has.'

'Good.' All at once Jenny slumped down in a chair. 'I didn't go far in case you needed help.'

'It was only a chat.'

'*Chat?*' Jenny cried scornfully. 'You couldn't have a proper chat with that lady. She looked terrific but she sounded pretty tough.'

'I have a feeling she's had a pretty tough life,' Dana said.

'If she has, it doesn't show.' At seventeen, Jenny saw a lot of things in the light of clothes. 'That outfit she had on was fabulous!'

'Fabulous indeed. I happen to know she bought it from Sonia Eden.'

'Gosh!' Jenny exclaimed loudly. 'I could never go in there.'

And I don't think I will again, Dana thought. Being the subject of gossip made her feel very vulnerable. Even pressed, there had been no need for Sonia to supply so much information. Of course she had known Jay Benson was staying at Merrilands. Assumed like everybody else that she was having an affair with Nick.

'Before I forget,' Jenny informed her, 'the sofas will be ready on Monday.'

'Good. I'll ring Mrs Winterman to make sure she'll be at home.'

'Harry's wife's back,' Jenny told her casually. 'She didn't seem to like life on the run.'

'She only thought the grass was greener on the other side of the fence.'

'Oh yes.'

Dana was sitting under the ray-lamp when Nick rang that evening. The sound of his voice on the phone, the first time in four years, had the effect of making her eyes glow and her skin lose colour.

'Oh, hello, Nick.' She sat down hastily.

'How's the shoulder?'

'I won't forget that little incident in a hurry, but it's a lot better.'

'Good.' He sounded very businesslike and forceful. A man in a hurry. 'I have to fly back tomorrow or stand to lose a lot of money. I know it's short notice, but I guess you can throw a few things in a bag.'

'What are you talking about, Nick?' she asked, and her voice shook in nervous tension.

'I want you to come with me.'

'No thanks.'

'Listen,' he urged. 'You know you *have* to.'

'I don't have to do anything.' She shook her head.

'You can't defer it much longer, Dana, or you'll never get in a light plane again.'

'Does it matter?' She could feel her nerve dissolving.

'It's getting late and I've got a lot to do,' he answered. 'I'll pick you up at seven sharp. You ought to be able to take a few days off.'

'Nick!' she called weakly, but he had already hung up.

Even the simple matter of strapping herself into the seat seemed a very arduous manoeuvre.

'Come on, now, Dana, *relax*,' ordered Nick.

Her small knuckles showed white.

'It's a good day for flying.'

'I don't want to hear about it.'

'Then look out the window. It's the best view of Merrilands.'

Dana looked, trying to calm the intense agitation in her mind. Once she had loved flying, riding through the sky, now the thought of what had happened to her father froze her in her seat.

'I'm beginning to think I can never take a holiday,' he said conversationally as the twin-engined plane thrust up into the sky. 'The slightest malfunction and it's a great big deal.'

Dana started to concentrate on what he was saying intensely. 'Something wrong?'

'A section of software not working correctly. A malfunction or breakdown in a system can cost an awful lot of time and money.'

'Haven't you people you can call in?'

'Darling,' he gave her a black, sideways glance,

'*I'm* people. I'd like to know I had a lot of bright boys to rely on, yet I get the impression that if anything happened to me at least two of my companies would go *pffft!*'

'It must be rather crushing, the responsibility?'

'I can take it. For now,' he said hardly.

'What do you want with Merrilands, Nick?' Finally her heartbeat was slowing.

'I told you. The day you threw me out was the day I decided I'd buy it for a joke.'

Bright sunlight flooded the plane and she turned her head to stare at his rugged profile. 'I wasn't in control of myself that day.'

'Are you in control of yourself now?'

'I think so.' She swallowed. 'I don't feel like screaming.'

'Terrors have a way of fading when we face them.'

'I couldn't have faced it without *you*.'

'I believe you.'

'You're such a tyrant,' she sighed.

'What else is there in life?' There was a faint smile on his devastating face. 'Does Jenny feel equal to looking after the shop?'

'I'll be back on Monday.'

'That's interesting. I have something planned for Monday.'

'*Monday*, Nick,' she said again.

'Have you forgotten I'm your client and this is without question your biggest job?'

'So what do you want me to do?' she exclaimed.

'I thought, if I'm able, we might take a tour of the galleries, buy a few paintings. Buying paintings has been a mild obsession of mine.'

'I suppose you got that from your mother,'

Dana reflected gently. 'She used to love the paintings in the house. I used to find her standing looking at the pictures she especially loved—the mysterious quality of the Impressionist school.'

'God, what a life she had!' Nick sighed. 'I could have given her the world, but she couldn't stay with me.'

'You really loved one another, didn't you?' Dana commented.

'The thing I can't forget is how little I was able to do for her. Here I am, a great big success, even by your father's standards, and it doesn't seem to mean very much. I'm rich and I get richer, but I can't really appreciate it. What gifts are mine I can't even count highly. Matching my best against the best and coming out on top only gives me a passing pleasure. What I really wanted to do was make it all up to my mother, yet I could give her nothing. She died in poverty.'

More than anything else in the world she wanted to comfort him. 'Far from it, Nick,' she said emotionally. She waited a moment, then spoke again. 'She had *you*. Don't you remember the delight you gave her? She was so proud of you.'

'Isn't that ridiculous?'

'She knew what you would become. We all did. I think she's looking down at you right now.'

'Then she wouldn't approve of what I'm doing,' he said sombrely. 'Count on it.'

'Then why are you doing it?' she asked with an odd simplicity.

'Because, darling,' he glanced at her, 'I'm not my sweet, selfless little mother. Losing her was the beginning of my total ruthlessness. *I'm* driven by demons, all of them determined on taking you over.'

'Is it possible to hate so much someone you once loved?'

'Sometimes hating is important,' said Nick. 'I don't think I could have made it any other way.'

There was a car waiting to meet them at the airport driven by a company executive, and as Nick almost immediately started talking business, Dana could sit back and relax her mind. In one way it had been a smooth, uneventful flight, in another, a giant step forward in her self-destruction. A demon really was prowling around somewhere inside Nick. Very occasionally she saw it looking at her out of his eyes. She only thought she knew what sort of childhood he had had. All she did know was that he had eaten his heart out for his mother. Men like Nick, physically powerful men, were often the most protective towards women, and never being able to grant his mother the comfort she so richly deserved had left its mark. He was a man who projected a bold and self-sufficient image, yet he had loved two women with an intensity few understood.

She was set down at the Hilton Hotel and Nick told her briefly he would ring her. She wondered again at the vast differences in him. He had always conveyed an incredible, quite natural quality of intellectual superiority, now he was the man whose every order was executed in great haste. She had particularly noticed the quality of attention his top executive was giving him. It revealed a great deal. Nick had become a man of power, and therefore a man to be feared.

In the afternoon she bought the piano she wanted, a superb concert grand, and made arrangements for it to be transported to Merrilands the following week.

'Still keeping up your playing, I see, Miss Merriman?' a senior member of the family-owned company boomed, hurrying forward to shake her hand.

Small wonder he was glad to see her, Dana thought. The piano had cost a fortune, though Nick had seemed unsurprised by the approximate prices she had quoted. She would have to make certain Mrs Owens worked the keyboard every day, even if it was only to press down on it with a duster. Magnificent instruments like the Steinway deserved a great deal better than being treated as a piece of sculpture, but Nick had told her what he wanted.

'Every house should have a piano,' he had said even as she argued away about the lack of a pianist without success.

'You may enjoy coming over from time to time,' he had suggested, not even bothering to conceal his mockery. She had enjoyed every material advantage, taking it as her due. The Merriman men had expected their women to have accomplishments. Really, Dana suspected, they were only chosen from a background that ensured they knew how to behave. Her parents' marriage, she had learned from Uncle Arthur, stunned, had been more a marriage of great suitability than a genuine love match. How did such things happen? She would rather be lonely all her life than marry a man she could not love with her whole heart. And certainly he had to love her too—not determined on dragging her down into a hell of passion.

Later on she did a little shopping, then called in on Guy Ellis, the most exclusive and most expensive interior designer in the country.

'Dana!' He held her and kissed her in unfeigned pleasure. 'What a surprise!'

'I couldn't visit Sydney without calling in on you,' she smiled.

'I should think not!' He kept his arm around her, guiding her into his luxurious office. 'Now what on earth are you doing here?'

'Buying Steinways.' She sank into an ultra-modern, deeply comfortable chair, smiling disarmingly.

'Of course—I remember, you play.'

'It's not for me.' Dana crossed her slender long legs. 'A client.'

'Oh?' Guy, a handsome, middle-aged man with blue, twinkling eyes, put his head on the side. 'Would that be Nick McMasters?'

'Is there anything you don't know?' she groaned.

'Oh dear!' Guy steepled his fingers in mild consternation. 'Of course I know Nick. Who doesn't? As a matter of fact I've done a lot of work for him, at the penthouse and at his main offices. Mercifully we saw eye to eye. Not an easy man to please, Nick, and very demanding. I used to say to him, there's a limit to what most people can do, but of course he doesn't care about or notice most people. He's a law unto himself.'

'Yes.' Despite herself Dana sighed. 'Curious how a handful have ten times more energy than is even granted to the strong.'

'That's why he's so successful, of course.' Guy's blue eyes were reflective. 'Sometimes I used to think, though, he didn't have much peace of the spirit. This could happen to great achievers. Then again, there was you.'

'Don't blame me, Guy.' Dana willed her voice to remain light and normal.

'My dear, I couldn't blame you for anything. As for Nick? I don't know. I have the feeling if one hurt him he would find it difficult to forgive.'

'He owns Merrilands, of course.' Dana raised her violet, black-lashed eyes.

'I know. How can you stand it?'

'I honestly don't know how I've stood anything that's happened in the past four or five years.'

'You're a brave girl, Dana,' Guy nodded his silvered head several times. 'When we first met years ago when you were only a teenager you had the world at your feet. I never saw a lovelier, more adored creature. I was shocked out of my mind when your father was killed. Then to lose your home, your heritage. It must have been terrible!'

'Yes, Guy.' What she didn't say was: It was worse to lose Nick.

'Have dinner with me tonight?' Guy insisted.

'If you want to. That would be lovely.' She thought suddenly of Nick and his reaction to such arrangements.

'You know I wanted you to work for me here?'

'I know your advice and encouragement started me off.'

'And you're wasted in the country,' Guy smiled. 'I hear so many reports of you. All glowing—but then your elegance was bred in the bone.'

The telephone rang—Guy's head designer— then afterwards they had coffee and Guy showed her around the showroom, both of them immersed in talking shop. Guy was a trained architect, strayed into the interior design business wherein he had made a fortune. Dana felt like a schoolgirl beside him, which wasn't surprising as Guy had always been her guiding light. These days, Guy's clients, of necessity, were very wealthy with fine collections for Guy to work with, but Dana knew, as did everyone else in the business, what Guy could do with only a modest budget. He was a remarkably talented and actually beloved man. Many another successful interior designer owed a lot to his private counselling.

'Now here's something that might interest you for Merrilands.' Guy bent down and opened out a huge box. 'Louis XV.'

'What is it?' she asked.

'Take a look, dear,' Guy said gently. 'Shockingly expensive but otherwise exquisite. It would be glorious at Merrilands, with those wonderful high ceilings.'

The box contained a magnificent rose quartz and rock crystal chandelier.

'Wherever did you get that?' Dana murmured.

'My man in London. My dear girl, I can't tell you my sources. Marvellous, isn't it, but as I say, a staggering price.'

'How much?'

Guy told her and Dana laughed gaily. 'You'll want a millionaire!'

'We've got one,' Guy retorted, widening his eyes. 'Our Nick.'

When Dana arrived back at the hotel she was told there had been two phone calls but no messages. Nick rang again when she was in the shower.

She padded out to the phone, clutching the towel around her.

'So you're back?' Nick's voice said briskly.

'For a little while.'

'What does that mean?'

'I'm going out to dinner.' Her knees knocked together.

His sharp laugh caught her off guard. 'What are you talking about, Dana?'

'I'm going out to dinner with a friend. You know him—Guy Ellis.'

'Well,' he said unexpectedly, 'have a good time.'

'I shall, thank you.' Her voice sounded very soft and anxious to please. 'Did you correct your problem?'

'We'll be working here all night,' he told her.

'*All* night?'

'Unless I have a brainwave. Which is always possible.'

She stood quietly. 'I hope so, Nick.'

'I've contacted a gallery to give us a private showing Sunday, is that all right?'

'I never expected you to consult me.'

'Just as well. And much worse, darling. You're coming to a dinner party with me tomorrow night.'

'Please, Nick, do I *have* to?' Damp towel and all, she sank on to the bed.

'As a matter of fact, yes. I promise not to upset, trample or dominate you in any way.'

'You're not going to find that very easy,' she commented.

'Possibly. But I'm going to make the effort. I was hoping I wouldn't be tied up here, but I am. That's the worst thing about being your own boss—you can't expect other people to solve your problems.'

'No.' Dana glanced down at her bare, curling toes. 'What time do you want me to be ready, Nick?'

'I'll pick you up at seven-thirty. If you haven't brought a dinner dress, you'd better get one. I want to flaunt you.'

'Oh, Nick, for God's sake, *why*?'

'You *know* why, darling,' he said harshly, and rang off.

CHAPTER SEVEN

SATURDAY morning she had early breakfast in her room and was at a hairdressers ten minutes after the salon opened.

'What are you doing with this beautiful hair long?' Her hairdresser, the owner and an expert, held long tresses away from her head. 'You're dragging out all the curl.'

'Long it's so easy to keep in a smooth shape,' Dana explained.

He clicked his tongue disgustedly. 'I make a fortune in perms and here you are tucking your beautiful curly hair out of sight! If you'll allow me to cut it, I'll literally transform you. You're a beautiful girl, but I can make you positively ravishing. What I have in mind is a marvellous style.' He clasped his hands tight to her head. 'Your face is a perfect oval, so I propose a centre part.' Next he dug his fingers into her hair and began sweeping her hair up and out. 'You're not making the best of yourself. This hair should be layered to set it free. It's superb hair, thick with a deep wave. I find the majority of women haven't got a clue what suits them best.'

So spoken to, there was nothing else for Dana to do but listen. She nodded her head and he smiled at her, acknowledging her good sense, and a few minutes later long black tresses began to fall around her.

They brought her a cold orange drink in a frosted glass, and she gazed at herself in wonderment. An extravagant dark cloud of hair offset her small face, winging back and upwards much as it had done in what seemed to her a century ago.

'You look wonderful!' the girl who had washed her hair told her. 'I'd give anything for those glorious waves!'

As it was, Dana gave a good deal, but it was worth it. 'All my clients leave the salon looking their best,' her hairdresser told her. 'Never go back to wearing your hair long again.'

Shopping around for a dinner dress it was very difficult to get used to her new image, let alone the extraordinary lightness of her head. Catching sight of herself in mirrors, she was carried back years, and knew a moment of feverish excitement not untouched by terror. Her cool, poised look had completely disappeared. She looked a young girl with a young girl's delicate uncertainty.

'Good heavens, dear, how did you do that?' the assistant in the third boutique cried.

'A ladder fell on me.'

'It must hurt?'

'No, not really. Not any more.'

'What a pity,' the woman said. 'We'll have to cover your shoulders. Otherwise I had just the thing.'

Eventually they found it—a rustly silk taffeta in the most beautiful shade of hyacinth.

'You can leave the front buttons open as low as you like.'

'I think we'll do *that* one up,' Dana said. The extended sleeve lent the necessary few inches to her shoulder, the V neck was delicately self-ruffled, the waist was tiny, cinched by a glittering belt, and the skirt formed a bell. She needed shoes to go with it, as well, and the right shade of stockings. The silver evening bag she had brought with her would match the glitter on the belt.

She was dressed by seven that evening and shaking with nerves. The mirror told her she looked very beautiful but oddly vulnerable. She looked little more than nineteen or twenty, but strangely this gave her no pleasure. This was the way she had looked before, deep, deep, deeply in love.

She turned on the television, trying to calm herself, then at five minutes short of the appointed time, she took the lift to the lobby, though she knew Nick would come up for her. Instead she knew she had to arrest his attention. Nick was dangerous, and looking as she did she knew she was threatened.

'Dana?'

She was sitting in a pool of light, oblivious to the avidly admiring glances.

'Oh, Nick.' She gave him her hand. 'I thought I'd come down and wait for you.'

His eyes were travelling all over her, and suddenly she was seized with fright. 'I've had my hair cut.'

He didn't answer, but it seemed to her that his dark golden skin had gone a shade paler.

'Do you like it?' She tried gently, ineffectually to release her hand.

'It's a hell of a time to ask me!'

Dana wasn't certain if it was rage or desire she saw in his eyes. 'How was your day? I hope you got everything straightened out?'

'Of course.' He took her arm. 'Come along, Dana, I can't hold the parking space for long.'

Even when they had left the city she was still swallowing nervously. 'Where are we going?' she asked.

'The Kidstons'. Sir Bernard has put a lot of work my way.'

'And they're expecting *me*?'

'They're expecting Grant Merriman's daughter. Your father and Sir Bernard were old school friends.'

In fact Dana was received with the greatest warmth and hospitality. Sir Bernard Kidston looked what he was; a man of vast wealth and ambition. A tough man, really, but he was delighted to greet Dana.

'You have a strong look of your father, my dear.' He took her hand and smiled. 'Looking at you I can see him as he was as a young boy. He had those remarkable blue eyes. But they're not blue, are they? A deep jacaranda?'

There were twenty people to dinner, all of whom obviously knew Nick well. The food was superb, as were the wines, and the conversation ranged over a good many subjects both serious and amusing.

Dana had little difficulty keeping her end up. The things they spoke of were much the same sort of things she had been used to all her life: art, politics, current issues, personalities, and then the antics of the domestic robot Nick had engineered for Sir Bernard's amusement.

'I have difficulty remembering he's not human,' Lady Kidston told them.

'But I want to see him!' one of the women guests demanded.

'And so you shall!' Sir Bernard was well prepared.

Moments later a square silver robot perhaps five feet tall was summoned by remote control, walking stiffly up to Sir Bernard, arms outstretched.

'I want you, Zoran, to remove the dishes from the table.' Sir Bernard added a little verbal drama to the manipulation of the buttons.

'Oooh!' The same woman who had expressed her curiosity lifted her hands in mock alarm.

The robot removed Sir Bernard's empty dinner plate and placed it on the trolley a female staff member quickly rolled forward. Dana noticed she was watching the robot with an expression of human affection, while the guests looked on fascinated.

The performance kept up along the table without the slightest mishap.

'What else can he do? Can I get one? Nick?'

'He can help you hang the curtains,' Lady Kidston answered quite seriously. 'He can vacuum. He can even answer the door. Bernie does it, of course, when he feels like a great laugh.'

'Nothing to the one you're working on, is it, Nick?' Sir Bernard said with enthusiasm. 'Some device to emulate a sense of balance. Zoran here can't correct his own balance. Can you, old fellow?'

'It will come,' said Nick. 'I expect to perfect a control mechanism to allow great precision and predictability of robotic movement. Zoran was designed basically to give Bernard a good deal of fun.'

'No, he *can't* come to you, Virginia.' Lady Kidston chuckled affectionately, looking down at her friend.

'I was thinking for a party, you know.'

'*No!*'

By the time the men went off to talk the inevitable business they were all wonderfully relaxed and laughing.

'I've never seen anything like it outside that *Star Wars*,' Virginia Sewell said to Dana as they were touching up their make-up. 'Honestly, Nick's the most brilliant man! Bernie gave him his start, but I shouldn't be surprised if Nick will be favouring Bernie some day. Have you known Nick long?'

'Twenty years.'

'Why, that's impossible!' Virginia exclaimed in gentle astonishment. 'Unless he's known you all your life.'

'Just about. I'm twenty-six.'

'My goodness, *are* you?' The woman peered at her. 'Dazzling creature! Of course Nick always has some stunning female in tow, but you're entirely different.'

'Really?' Dana said reservedly.

'I say, I haven't put my foot in it, have I, dear?'

'Good heavens, no,' Dana said calmly. 'Nick and I are just good friends.'

Mrs Sewell threw back her head and roared. 'Friends? That's good! I know I'm shortsighed, dear, but a blind woman could see Nick has taken a great fancy to you. And that's really something from a man who gives nothing away. By the way a man looks at you, you shall know. My God, I wish I'd met a man like that just once in my life—but I suppose they wouldn't make the easiest companions. I adore my Billy, but he's never been the stuff of passion.'

The men emerged from the library after about an hour and shortly after midnight the party broke up.

'I'll see you again, won't I, my dear?' Sir Bernard said.

'Of course you will,' Nick answered for her without the faintest qualm. 'Lovely evening, Clare,' he kissed Lady Kidston's cheek.

'I guessed right, then?' she asked him.

'What was all that about?' Dana asked him when they were in the car.

'I can't remember now.'

'Are you sure?'

'Absolutely.'

'I thought it had something to do with me.'

'You flatter yourself, darling,' Nick drawled.

'Anyway, I did enjoy myself.' She leant her head back.

'You were a great success.'

'Wasn't that said rather fiercely?' She swung her head abruptly.

'Sorry. I only meant it in the nicest possible way.'

The mockery in his tone made her avert her head.

'I remember you wore a dress almost that colour the night we became engaged,' he added.

It was too dim to see his face, but his voice sounded sombre and slightly hostile.

'I'd forgotten,' sighed Dana.

'I wonder.'

'All right, I remembered you love this colour.' Her body that had been so relaxed was now pierced with tension.

'You look not a minute different from what you looked then. Maybe more beautiful, because you've known pain.'

'You must be tired, Nick,' she said. 'I heard you tell someone you worked through until two this morning.'

'I'm not in the least tired. I never sleep more than a few hours. I don't need it.'

'I thought you were. . . .'

'Overdrawn?'

'A little.'

'I'm sure what you're really trying to say is you want me to drive you straight back to the hotel?'

'Surely you're going to?'

'How anxious you sound! No, darling, I don't approve of making love in hotel rooms.'

'I don't approve of being made love to forcibly either,' Dana assured him.

'Then you've changed a lot in the last few years.'

'Please, Nick, this is ill-advised.' To her dismay her voice trembled.

'I prefer to think it inevitable. There's nothing to be afraid of, Dana. I want you terribly and I'm going to have you.'

He spoke scarcely another word to her until they were inside the door of his penthouse apartment, and as she attempted to recover some element of normality he pulled her into his arms with a kind of ruthless energy and covered her trembling mouth with his own.

'No,' Nick!'

Her feeble protest was the fuse that lit an uncontrollable flare-up of passion. He lifted her off the floor as though she were still a child, and though she tried hard to control the answering frenzy that was in her her body was instantly in a high state of arousal. It even seemed to her she was leaping towards him even as she was frantically straining away from him, blindly arching her back.

'No, Dana, it won't do.' He held her harder still, his vastly superior strength locking her to him. 'Do you think I need all this drama? I know what you want.'

'What I want is over!' She shuddered violently, her violet eyes filled with tears.

He stopped her with his mouth, kissing her so deeply she had to lie absolutely still. It was monstrous the way her body betrayed her. Monstrous to want something so desperately, every defence mechanism was hopelessly overwhelmed.

When Nick lifted his mouth from hers he was groaning faintly and she could do no more than try to gasp some air into her famished lungs. All of it, from the beginning, had been beyond her control. His hands turned her, disengaged the lovely dress from her body.

She began to cry, very softly.

'Don't, darling!' Nick begged.

'I can't help it.'

'I wish to God I could. You're beautiful—*so* beautiful. It doesn't seem possible I could want to punish you.'

His hands palmed her breasts, then when she made little helpless moaning sounds, he slid his hand beneath her slip and wisp of bra and teased the nipple, the pressure hardening until her eyelids fluttered and finally lay still. *Nick*. He had always had that power. Knew everything about her.

Moments passed while he concentrated on caressing her, curled in his lap. There was enormous feeling flowing between them, a rush of memory from another time.

'Nick?' Dana whispered unsteadily, without opening her eyes.

'Strange, isn't it?' he said. 'I've always been desperately hungry for you.' He held her face up to him and kissed her mouth.

It was a plunge into an infinite void where she had no hold on her weightless, fluttering body or her faltering mind.

'Nick!' she protested in a feverish, frightened way, and he lifted her, carrying her into the bedroom and lowering her on to the bed, where she lay turned on her side with one arm stretched out.

'Nothing changes, does it?' He sat down behind her, cupping his hands on her naked breasts. 'Four years ago, Dana, you left me bereft. It's impossible to forget what it's been like.'

'Oh, you've forgotten,' she said jaggedly. 'Woman after woman.'

He turned her, angling the bedside lamp so it played over the glistening dark cloud of her hair and her intensely white skin.

'And what about you?' His black eyes were more eloquent than any warning.

'You mean you *want* to hear?'

'Go ahead.'

'Once I descended into a desperate experiment. It didn't work. It was nothing.'

'Who was he?' He was totally absorbed in what she was saying.

Dana shook her head, dismissing a brief hour of human weakness. 'It meant a lot to him, so I was sorry.'

'O.K. Do I know him?'

'Yes. He was always in love with me.'

'I thought so.' His curvy mouth fined down to a hard line. 'It was probably Dan Newell.'

'An exceptional guess,' she sighed.

'Why the hell did you have to do it to poor old Dan?'

'Is that a reprimand?' Dana turned her head into the bank of pillows.

'You know full well Dan had a crush on you from adolescence.'

'I didn't know, actually, for quite a while. I never saw anyone else but your you. You were my daily life.'

'I just wish you hadn't called a squad of police to get rid of me.' Nick stood up and shouldered out of his half opened shirt, his powerful body superbly fit and hard. With the black tangle of hair on his chest and the buccaneer's moustache, he looked enormously virile, looking down at Dana from his commanding male height.

'This is wrong,' she protested, crossing her two hands over her breast.

'If it is I don't much care.' He moved on to the bed and reached for her. 'It's all talk with you, Dana.'

She couldn't stop herself. She hit him, her humiliation so intense it was almost unbearable.

'So we fight a little.'

Beside him she both looked and felt doll-like, but as he was only toying with her fragile strength she managed to tear herself out of his arms and make a leap for the door.

A rug skidded beneath her and she gave a sickened little moan, terribly frightened now that she was going to further injure her shoulder.

'Why must you do these stupid things?' He reached her before she fell flat, scooping her up into his arms.

'Let me go home, Nick,' she said in sudden exhaustion and sadness.

He shook his head. 'You're staying here, even if *I* have to put up on the sofa.'

'You're crazy,' she said frailly. 'You've always been crazy. You go your own way. It's your nature.'

'I won't touch you. I just want you here.'

'And what do we do in the morning? What do we do when Jay Benson calls?'

'Jay doesn't call on me. I call on her.'

It was astounding the multitude of sensations she felt. '*Please*, Nick.' She tried desperately to impress her will on his. 'All we're doing is hurting each other.'

He tried to smile, but he didn't quite make it. 'I don't know about you, but I don't mind a little hurting. After all, it must be *my* turn.' Now the male aggression was showing more clearly.

'All right,' she said raggedly. 'I got myself into this, now I can't get out.'

'All of us at some time or other are as helpless as rabbits.' From a hard ruthlessness he amazed her with an easy, relaxed smile. 'You can have the bed.'

'Am I to understand I'm a prisoner?'

'My guest.' He lowered her to her feet, but kept his arms around her. 'It's all right, darling, I'm no longer in a rage. Sometimes, just sometimes, you're my dear little sister. Like when you're about to fall over.'

'I have everything at the hotel, Nick!' she wailed.

'You don't need anything but a toothbrush, and I can give you a new one.'

'That's not exactly what I mean.' Both of them seemed unaware that they were in an advanced state of undress.

'I'll tell you what I'll do,' Nick offered. 'Some time in the morning I'll go around and get your things.'

'I don't want you to do that!' Her nerves were raging.

'It's no trouble. You have the bathroom first. I'll definitely need a cold shower.'

'Well, *goodnight*!' Dana called, a good twenty minutes later.

Nick came to the door of the bedroom in a short wine-red bath robe, his black hair damp from the shower and curling in little clusters. 'Want me to tuck you in?'

'You're enjoying this, aren't you, you monster?' She pummelled a plump pillow with her fist.

'I have an obsession to hear you breathe.'

She gazed at him quickly. 'Incredibly, you sound serious,' she said faintly.

'I used to keep myself awake watching you sleep.'

'*Stop it!*' In a minute she would start crying, helpless to stop.

'Goodnight, Dana,' he said quietly. 'Sleep deeply. I won't disturb you.'

About three o'clock her nightmare began. It was an old dream when the police called on her to tell her haltingly that her father had been killed. She could see them quite clearly. She remembered every word they said, but it had to be some appalling joke, because her father was still working in his study where she had left him. She slammed the door on the two policemen and rushed back through the entrance hall. There were flowers everywhere—wreaths and great urns. The light was on in the study and her father looked up at her.

'I knew you were there,' she was crying. 'I *knew* it!'

She came out of this dream and went into another. This time she knew her father was dead. There were people everywhere in the house, trying to talk to her and catch her hands. Somehow she had to get out, go to Nick. Nick would rescue her, end this torture. She was screaming his name so hoarsely she thought her lungs would burst.

'*Dana!*'

She was lying on her back with Nick holding her down.

'Ah!' She knew at once where she was.

'My God, you screamed as if you were dying!' he muttered.

'I was.' Her heart was beating painfully and the only way to quiet it was to press down on her breast.

'Lie quietly.' There was an expression of the utmost concern on his face.

'I was dreaming about the funeral,' she said jaggedly.

'Go on. It happens often?'

'It used to, but not for a long time.' Her violet eyes were glittering and she had a flush on her high cheekbones like a fever. 'I think our dreams frighten us just as much as reality. My heart is beating like a sledge hammer.'

'Yes.' His hand went to her breast, the rapid

action of her heart stirring the fine lace on her slip. 'I wonder if you should have a brandy to settle you.'

'No. Could I have a glass of water?'

He gave her a considering look. 'Odd how you can sound like a little girl.'

Dana had to control her impulse to burst into tears.

He was back in a moment and she drank the cold water down. 'Thank you.'

'You're trembling,' he said gently.

'Don't be nice to me, Nick,' she begged.

'You look so tragic it's rather difficult to be anything else.'

'I was looking for you,' she said.

'In your dream?' He sat down again on the side of the bed, staring at her intently.

'I can never get to you. *Never!*' she said with agitation. 'There are people everywhere trying to reach out for me.'

'And your father's in your dream?'

'At the beginning. There are police at the door assuring me he'd d-d. . . .' Her tongue caught and she burst into tears.

'Dana!' Nick shook his head sombrely and drew her into his arms.

'It was you I was trying to reach, Nick,' she told him.

'Why not? You belong to me.'

'But you're angry! You pretend not to be, but you are.'

'I have my ghastly nightmares as well,' he told her soberly.

'We can't sort this out, *can* we?' She tilted her head back, searching his black eyes.

'I want you to marry me,' he said.

'I *know* that, Nick. The terrible part is, I know why.'

'*Why?*' He caught her back against him, threading his hand through the springing mass of her hair. 'Because I'm half demented without you!'

She was seized with laughter, strange and unnatural. 'Demons—demented! You could hurt me dreadfully.' She kicked away the bedclothes with her arched foot. 'Go on,' she invited, 'hurt me. It will be like old times.'

The odd part was that she did this to him deliberately—provoked the violent male in him. In one devastating motion he turned his body to meet hers, an assault she craved so much it was almost a delirium. This was compulsion, a desire that had dominated their lives.

Her mouth met his with the same mania of longing and he held her so powerfully she had no recourse but to let her slender body melt into his. For four years she had endured a purgatory of self-denial, and now it was beyond her to refuse a conquest that was ordained.

Some time before dawn Nick woke her slowly and made love to her again. Not with the taste of fury that was almost a pagan ritual but with a shattering sweetness, a desire that seemed limitless. When she raced ahead, he slowed her, controlling her responses so that she began to think his mastery was not quite human, but of a higher order. Where else had he learnt this extraordinary power?

'Be my wife,' he urged her when she was irretrievably lost.

'Can't you say you love me?' Dana opened her weighted eyes, looking up at him wildly.

'I'll say anything you want.' His tongue tasted and teased her yearning body.

'Nick, don't stop!' she begged.

'You've got to marry me. *Promise!*'

'I ... I ... I ....' It was an agonised, accelerating little cry.

'*Say* it.' He watched her, tormenting and soothing.

'I'll marry you,' she said faintly.

'When?'

'Whenever you like.'

'*This* time you will.'

Her fingernails sank into his powerful back.

'There, there, everything is all right.' Nick buried his face between her breasts, then sought her trembling, defenceless mouth.

She had thought they had touched the pinnacle of desire, but now she understood there were extremes of ecstasy.

I'm going away, she thought. Dying of rapture.

Tiny wings were fluttering all over her body, now spreading, opening wide. She seemed to be vibrating with that rush of power. Now she was soaring, soaring in a trail of glory, a speck in the sky, winging in a floating arc towards a terrible, brilliant brightness.

The excitement was more than she could possibly absorb. She wasn't even conscious she cried Nick's name. Her body went into its own triumphant spasm, explosions of stars colouring the world around them. She wanted to hold on to the moment, exult in it forever, but the mind had to acknowledge the body's frailty.

While Nick held her, his own heart pounding in a rival panic, she gave the familiar little keening cry that still floated in his memory and slipped away.

He knew she had fainted. He was still trying to absorb the shock of his own passion. He lay on his side and gathered her into him, while her head fell like a child's on to his shoulder.

'You're *mine*,' he said, and his tone wasn't tender, but hard and declarative.

CHAPTER EIGHT

THE placement of the paintings necessitated a certain amount of rearranging, but Dana hadn't enjoyed anything so much in years.

'Isn't that beautiful, now!' Mrs Owens said of a huge portrait of a lady being centred in the drawing room. 'She has a look of you, Miss Dana.'

'That's what Nick thought.' The portrait by Jacques Emile Blanche was quite exceptional, executed with a great deal of panache. 'Paintings and sculptures, art objects really make a home. Without the owners' things everything tends to look dead.'

'You must have spent a fortune!' Mrs Owens trusted herself to say.

'Good buys, every one of them,' Dana told her, gesturing to her workmen to tilt the painting a little to the left. 'Paintings of this quality only move up in price, not down.'

'I know nothing about paintings,' Mrs Owens said 'but it seems to me everything you've brought back is beautiful.'

'Mr McMasters made the choices. I only sat around agreeing. Some of these paintings and a couple of the sculptures he already had.'

'I've never enjoyed a place so much in my life!' Mrs Owens' round pink face looked her pleasure. 'I can't wait for the grand opening. Mr McMasters said he's going to throw a big party.'

'Yes.' Dana felt a little stab of panic. A pre-wedding party, though it was far too early to tell Mrs Owens that. She had given Nick her promise even if she had been off her mind, and it was not a promise she could withdraw. Another rejection, she thought quite helplessly, might cost her her life.

'About the statue, now?' Ted Allen, the workman, came down the ladder. 'I'll need a hand with that.'

'Bill's around some place,' Dana came back to reality with a jolt.

'Bill will do very well. What *is* it, for instance?'

'You can't see?'

When she walked into the library Mario, with the help of his two nephews, had the ceiling-high bookcases flanking the fireplace in place.

'Oh, they're superb, Mario!' Dana exclaimed.

'Yesa, that's right. I tell you no one's as good a craftsman as me.'

'Not many, Uncle.'

'*No one.*' Mario turned his head, and his stocky young nephew seemed to squirm.

'If you say so, Uncle.'

Dana dared not intervene. Both young men worked for their uncle in any case, and from what Dana had seen of their work in cabinetmaking, they were certain to make a very comfortable living.

When she returned to the shop, late afternoon, Jenny seemed greatly relieved. 'Mr Vaughn called in at lunchtime and he's rung twice this afternoon,' she told Dana.

'I'll take care of it, Jenny.'

'He was terribly stiff and stern,' Jenny babbled. 'The second time he rang he just hung up on me.'

'Perhaps it was an accident?'

'No accident,' Jenny replied. 'He sounded terribly annoyed.' Her large eyes were very bright and curious. 'I suppose you're trying to give him the brush?'

'*My* business again, Jenny.' Dana looked down at her messages.

'Not that there's actually anything wrong with him,' Jenny mused. 'He just seems more like your father than your boy-friend.'

'Did Mr Ralston call?' Dana looked up, her expression indicating she wished to talk business.

'He did.' Jenny hurried to her table. 'He said he had an exclusive new collection to show you.'

'And when is this?'

'Let's see.' Jenny wallowed around for a moment. 'Ah, here it is. Ten Thursday morning, if that's all right.'

'Okay. Now here are a few phone calls I want you to make, then you can run off home.'

An hour later, Dana was sitting with Keith having a quiet drink. Or endeavouring to.

'I mean, Dana, is it out of sight, out of mind?'

'I'm sorry, Keith.' She had apologised for the third time.

'Hell!' Keith was still indignant and aggrieved. 'I can't take this sort of thing, you know. Actually I wonder if you care about me at all.'

She knew full well she had to tell him. 'I do care about you, Keith,' she said gently, 'but not in the way you want.'

'You're just amusing yourself, do you mean?' His fine skin filled with colour.

'Certainly not!' She was glad there were only a few people scattered around the large lounge. 'I don't love you, Keith, that's the whole point.'

'Love! What a lot of drivel!'

'But it *isn't*, is it?' she said wryly.

He put out his hand to cover hers. 'I have enough love for both of us.'

She shook her head. 'You can't seriously believe something like that would work?'

'You silly creature! You're just afraid of love,' Keith told her.

'No,' she raised her eyes. 'I'm going to marry Nick McMasters, Keith,' she said abruptly.

'What *is* this?' He tightened his grip painfully on her hand. 'Some infernal punishment he's drummed up. I've found out a lot about this McMasters. There's nothing to be afraid of. I'll protect you.'

'I've given him my promise, Keith,' she said.

'So?' A muscle jerked along his jawline. 'Break it. Like you did before.' As soon as he said it, he was utterly dismayed. 'Dana dearest, you know what I mean,' he murmured wretchedly. 'You did the right thing before and you'll do it again. Tell me the truth. He has some hold on you, hasn't he?'

'Inexorably.' Dana's violet eyes were beautiful and disturbed. 'It's all my fault, Keith, but I've tried to be honest with you. I've enjoyed your companionship very much. We've had some delightful times, but one can't love at will, any more than one can destroy it.'

'You mean you love him?' Keith asked angrily.

'It's something beyond loving.'

'You little fool!' For the first time his good-looking face looked ugly. 'You ought to find yourself a psychiatrist and get yourself straightened out!'

'I expect you could do with a few visits as well.'

'I can't accept this,' said Keith, closing his eyes. 'All this is one of his fiendish schemes! A crude plan even a child could work out. He had a difficult childhood, didn't he? Almost everyone in this town has had a story to tell me. So he was brilliant? I'd say his experiences have twisted his mind.'

'You can always count on experiences to do that.'

He stared at her, his fingers closing over her elbow, once more. 'They say he had a breakdown after his mother died?'

'He had a very hard time.'

'You lost *your* father, Dana,' Keith pointed out. 'Did you go to pieces?'

'So many pieces I lost count.'

'So you're going to defend him?'

'The old story,' she sighed.

'You know, Dana, you don't look as if you're in your right mind,' Keith said severely. 'And what you've done to your hair is very interesting.'

'You don't like it?'

'Do you really want me to tell you what I think?'

'You're going to, anyway.'

'You're trying to go back to the past, and it's not safe. McMasters has a quality of violence—you know this yourself. You evidently didn't think yourself safe when you called the police to the house.'

'You've been doing a great deal of talking, haven't you, Keith?' she asked austerely.

'I've only been thinking of *you*. Anyway, it's quite natural for people to talk. Everyone has some incident to tell. They say he stopped two burly policemen in their tracks.'

Dana laughed oddly. 'They didn't hold it against him.'

'Really?' Keith's blue eyes turned icy. 'It's my understanding he was flung in jail—for *your* protection.'

'I was mad with grief.' She turned her head and looked away. 'Both of us in our way were victims, manipulated from beyond the grave.'

Keith looked back at her as if she had taken leave of her senses. 'Dana, *why?*' he cried. 'You can't marry McMasters! You're not that strong. He'll break you as soon as he gets the chance—I told you, I've made enquiries. He has only been in business a handful of years yet already he's some kind of a legend. What he wants, he goes after. The money doesn't even seem to be important. Wanting things is an imperative, and he wants *you*. I suppose he started to want you when you were only a child. His life's ambition—to be rich, to own a fine house and marry the girl that came with it. It's an old, old story. It's been written about in books and plays. Self-made men are always ruthless and grasping.'

'I've known some pretty awful born-rich ones,' said Dana.

'He's buying you, you know that!' Keith exclaimed disgustedly. 'Can't you be honest with yourself for a moment? He's buying you just like he bought your home. It doesn't matter what *you* want. You and the house are all one. You're the package. He'll glory in having a beautiful, well-bred wife. You see if he doesn't bring up the Merriman connection all the time. People like the Merrimans were the aristocrats of this country, the landed gentry. McMasters is no more than a ruthlessly ambitious adventurer.'

'And a brilliant scientist as well.'

'All right, Dana,' Keith laughed hollowly. 'McMasters is not in love with you, but I am. That gives me rights. I'm not going to rest until I prove to you the kind of man he really is.'

She told Vicki, of course. Nick had been adamant that he wasn't going to wait.

'But that's fantastic, Dana!' Vicki started towards her and gave her a great big hug.

'Me, too.' Timmy thrust against their knees.

'You, too.' Dana bent down to him and he covered her face with lots of sweet, warm, faintly sticky kisses.

'Hold hard there, Dana!' Vicki laughed. 'If you ask me, my son is going to be quite a ladies' man.'

'Darling little thing!' Dana took a deep breath as soon as she was able.

'Come on, poppet,' Vicki grasped her son's hand. 'What about getting going on your Legos? Dana would love to see your rocket.'

'Daddy and me in space,' Timmy announced proudly.

Dana nodded. 'I'd love to see it, Timmy.'

'Okay.' Timmy smiled at her radiantly, then ran off to the playhouse his father had built for him in a well located spot in the garden. From the kitchen windows and the rear patio Vicki could keep her eye on him all the time

'But this is wonderful news!' Vicki took the subject up again as soon as Timmy had shot off. 'Wait until I tell Dave. He'll be as thrilled as I am.'

'I'm keeping it quiet for now, Vick.' Dana sank down into a wicker chair. 'So far only you and Keith know.'

'And what did *he* say?' Vicki joined her beneath the huge umbrella.

'He said he wouldn't rest until he proved what kind of a man Nick is.'

'Dammit, how would *he* know?' Vicki countered flatly. 'He's jealous, of course. Impossible to avoid it.'

'Apparently he's been talking to a lot of people,' Dana let her eyes roam over the beauty of the garden. Even the patio where they were sitting was ablaze with colour, all the flowers of summer growing profusely out of a variety of pots and planters. 'The garden is looking beautiful, Vicki. Whatever you work at, you're a success.'

'Not bad for a little gardener largely self-taught. Now, my girl, we're talking about *you*.' Vicki retrieved the conversation. 'People love to talk—you know that. They've always talked about *you*. You're our last link with greatness—the Merriman saga, etc. Now Nick is all the rage. The town loves celebrities, and none better than home-grown. When the town hears you two are finally going to get married, they'll go crazy.' Vicki smiled innocently, waved to Timmy who waved back, then looked at Dana. What she saw brought her up short. 'Dana dear, you look unhappy!'

'It's a little complicated, Vicki.'

Vicki waited a while, then she sighed. 'You know you two have had a sort of heroic drama. Please don't be shocked by anything I say. I love you, Dana, you know that. My dearest friend, Timmy's godmother. I know if anything happened to me, happened to *my* mother, you'd always be there for Timmy, but I've never understood why you chose to reject Nick. Dave and I always used to joke that you and Nick had the greatest love affair of the century, so we were all doubly shocked when you parted. I suspect your father had a little bit to do with it. He idolised you, and Nick was showing quite plainly he was going to take you away. If only he hadn't been a sick man it wouldn't have mattered so much, but you were so close. I expect he couldn't bear to be without you. Some parents are like that. We both know Dad was damn difficult with Dave, and I see *my* dad all the time.'

'My father wasn't a sick man, Vicki,' Dana said tonelessly.

'I don't understand. His heart?'

'There was nothing wrong with his heart,' Dana said flatly.

'Oh, God!'

'He got Uncle Arthur to fabricate a story, and in my loyalty I believed it,' said Dana.

'My dear!' Vicki exhaled sharply. 'I always remember thinking your father looked so well. But then a lot of people with heart conditions look quite healthy. Why didn't you tell me this before?'

'You have to understand. I've been trying to protect my father all along.' Dana's voice was almost a whisper.

'Did Nick know?' Vicki asked, after a long swallow.

'Nick guessed. It was very difficult to fool him about anything.'

'And what did you say?'

'I denied it. He was very cruel.'

'You mean he was fighting for his life.'

'I suppose so, Vick,' Dana whispered. 'The more he attacked my father, the more I attacked him. It wasn't a question of love—God knows I loved Nick. It was more a question of loyalty, and my father deserved my loyalty.'

'How?'

'You can't mean that, Vicki?' Dana gazed in near horror at her friend.

'We must discuss that, Dana. Your father was a wonderful man, but like the rest of us he had his human weaknesses. He deliberately set about wrecking your relationship with Nick. At that time everyone was agreed you two were perfect for one another. Even the circumstances were extraordinary. You might as well say you were destined for Nick since you were six years old. You were together nearly every day of your lives, and your father certainly approved of him then. He approved of anyone who could keep his daughter happy. Even me.'

'What do you mean, *even you*, Vicki!' Dana demanded.

'Since you mention it, we weren't exactly in the Merriman league,' Vicki explained. 'You never can understand snobbery, Dana, but it exists. Some of your other girl friends wouldn't even know me. A lot of rich people are arrogant. They stick to their own circle, but you chose your friends differently. I'm your best friend, but Nick was the greatest friend you ever had. You can't alter facts.'

'*Nick* has altered,' Dana said.

'Of course he has altered. We all change. You've changed yourself, Dana. You used to have such gaiety, such radiance, but that came to an end when your world shattered. You've even frightened me at times. You've seemed so sad and lost.'

'Nick doesn't love me,' Dana said. 'He never wants to let me go.'

'Who'd blame him!' Vicki said tersely, then her voice gentled. 'Nick does love you. He's always loved you since you were a child.'

'Only that much I'm sure of. He loved me then.'

'And now?'

'I don't think he even knows himself,' said Dana. 'What Keith says is partly true.'

'Oh, rubbish!' Vicki said vigorously. 'Keith doesn't even know Nick. What does he say, anyway?'

'That Nick is a ruthless, ambitious adventurer.'

'My eye!' Vicki's pretty face showed its anger and resentment. 'Ambitious, yes. Adventurer, no. Ruthless, *never*. Nick is capable of great feeling, great sensibility. He's had to overcome massive setbacks, so he's had to be strong, but ruthless!'

'Whatever it is, Vicki, it's killing me. You haven't seen Nick's other side. I don't think he will ever forgive what I did to him until his dying day. Neither will he let me forget it.'

'I don't believe that,' said Vicki. 'Have you never seen his eyes watching you?'

'I have,' Dana answered, her voice tight. 'There's another Nick prowling around inside I can't reach.'

'Have you *tried*?'

'What can I say?' Dana asked unsteadily, her violet eyes wide and glistening.

'Tell him all of it, Dana,' Vicki suggested, very gently. 'Tell him about your father.'

'Oh, Vicki, I *can't*!' Dana protested.

'Bring it out in the open.'

'I'd do the same again.' Dana dropped her head and the gleaming weight of her hair bobbed against her neck. 'He would know that as well. Maybe Daddy knew he would always be there between us.'

Maybe he did, Vicki thought, and the realisation struck her harshly. But whatever violence was in Nick's heart, he wanted Dana. And now he knew he would have her.

The photographs arrived a week later, addressed to the shop. They came in an ordinary large yellow envelope, and Dana shook them out at first casually, then with a dawning insecurity.

'Oh, *Nick*!' Her head bowed and she was grateful she was alone in the shop. Alone there was no need to hide her misery. And that was what it was. Not rage, or shock, or jealousy, but a profound and tragic acceptance.

The two people in the series of photographs spread out on her desk were well known to her: Nick and Jay Benson. In the first, they were coming out of a restaurant—Cellini's, she could see the name. Their heads were close together, not in the normal fashion, but in the fashion of a man and woman who meant a lot to each other. In the second they were standing on the footpath beside a Jaguar. Nick was holding Jay's hand. Both of them looked very intense and handsome. They could have been posing for the cover of a romantic novel. In the third, Nick's arms were close around her and it seemed as though the woman was crying. In the fourth, her hair was against his face and she was kissing his cheek. Perhaps tomorrow Dana would get photographs of them together in bed.

The phone rang that night several times, but Dana didn't answer. Nick's apparent betrayal wasn't a violation of any sacred love. It wasn't even a violation of her. It was the start of a life sentence. She knew the photographs had come from Keith, but she had contempt for his methods. It was obvious he had hired a private detective.

His voice on the phone next morning was half defiance, half plea. 'I had to do it, Dana, don't you see that? The man is a philanderer, and a pretty incompetent one, as well. Or maybe he's not even going to bother to be discreet. He might like that—to humiliate you in public.'

'Why don't you offer the photographs to the local newspaper, Keith?' she asked him with exactly the right amount of contempt.

'My dear, the whole country will know it soon enough! You need help, Dana, and you're going to listen to me. . . .'

Never. Dana put the receiver down and looked out across the street. The only chance she had was to disappear. How did one disappear? She began considering the ways to do it. She had built up a successful business, but that had to go. She would have to sell the house. She would have to make a fresh start in another country: England. The main branch of her family was there. They had always kept up the connection. She would need protection. Nick was not a man to cross. So many things! To walk away from her commission at Merrilands would be to alert him. Without conceit she knew it would bring a brutal reaction. Yet how could he expect her to go through with a marriage that was more a sin than a sacrament? It was Jay Benson he held so tenderly, after all. He might never ask her to marry him, but it was obvious he meant to hang on to her as a mistress, just as it was obvious Jay Benson intended to grab what she could get. Millionaires weren't all that thick on the ground, and ones who looked like Nick unbelievably scarce.

He surprised her by flying in unannounced, just as they had finished assembling the furniture in the main guestroom. The original four-poster was still there, and Dana had hung it with a light airy valance and draperies. Now she lingered as Ted and Bill moved off, her eye wandering and darting around, thinking what she could do further to enhance the overall design. All the bedrooms were so vast by ordinary standards they could take a lot of furniture. Perhaps a chest of drawers over by the French doors.

'Dana?'

His voice startled her so much it might have issued from a ghost.

'Oh, God, Nick, you startled me!' she exclaimed.

'You must have been very deep in thought?' He sounded very cool and unconcerned.

'You were the last person I expected.' Dana said it too sharply.

'It's very easy to believe that.' He walked towards her, held her head up and dropped a hard kiss on her mouth. 'From what I've seen downstairs you've been working extremely hard.'

'We all have.' She stepped back and looked away. 'Is there anything that doesn't meet with your approval?'

'My welcome.'

'You can't win 'em all.' She hadn't meant to say that.

'And who the hell do I want to win, but you?' He stared down at her in frowning concentration.

'Now's my chance to ask.'

'But, darling, you know,' he said abruptly. 'I've never wanted to marry anyone in my life but you. Which brings me to why I'm really here. I want you to organise our big party for Saturday week.'

Unaware, the swift colour rushed into her cheeks. 'Maybe I don't want a big party.'

'We're having one. You can ask as many people as you like. I'll have my own list. Maybe you'll want to fly caterers in?'

'We have excellent people here,' she reminded him.

'Whatever you think. You know so perfectly how to handle these things.' There was a sharp smile in his brilliant black eyes and she turned away bewildered.

'I'm not ready for it, Nick.'

'Why, you've done wonderfully well.' He moved behind her and placed his hands on her shoulders. 'Black tie—that goes without saying. Women love dressing up. I know I can count on you to look enchanting. Don't say you're not ready, darling. You *are*.' The sardonic underscoring in his voice was much less unsettling than the shift in his hands. They moved lightly, swiftly, encircling her breasts, the thumbs barely teasing the instantly erect peaks.

'*Nick*!' she warned, her breath shortening.

The action became stronger.

Dana turned her head and immediately his mouth came down on her neck. 'Don't kid yourself, my darling,' he said tautly. 'You want me as much as I want you.'

Suddenly, footsteps sounded along the hallway and Nick released her unhurriedly, flinging at her the final taunt. 'I think the ring should be a sapphire, don't you? I couldn't bear to buy another diamond.'

The words cut deep. As they were meant to.

CHAPTER NINE

THE people who crowded the house were lavish in their praise.

'Dana, you've done a wonderful job!'

Had they forgotten that she had lived here? That this was *her* home? Now Nick walked the great rooms, darkly, exotically handsome, his white smile mocking the extravagant blandishments. Evening clothes gave him an incredible glamour, and those old families who had once labelled him an upstart now had little difficulty adjusting to the new régime. Not that it really mattered. Dana would remain the mistress of the house in which she had been brought up. It was a love story the whole district had followed with interest and a historic property remained in the right hands.

Dana had worked exhaustively on the arrangements. On the house, on the flowers, on the lighting, on the enormous marquees that had been set up on the lawn. She had even hired a quite famous group of musicians to play the dance music in the blue and gold ballroom banked with ferns and hydrangeas. It could even be said she had worked with ferocity, for her strapless silk chiffon dress, white with silver appliqué and lace, had needed some last-minute alterations to make the bodice and the tiny waist fit more snugly.

'Don't lose any more weight,' Nick told her. 'I don't want to have to shake the sheets to find you!'

Tonight she wore his ring, an exquisite

sapphire surrounded by diamonds, and as if that were not enough a sunburst of pavé-set diamonds at her ears and a matching antique pendant in the shape of a heart swinging between her breasts.

'From me to you, on this unforgettable occasion.'

She could still feel the warmth of his hands searing her soft skin. Everything had an underlying taunt to it. Barbed reminders. It seemed peculiar that she had worked so hard, or could be tortured by so many little things. She didn't even resent the overt flirtatiousness of many of the women guests with Nick. She had never had that sense of possession that brought on anger and jealousy. She had always felt if a man loved you there was nothing to be gained by constant vigilance. No one owned anybody, but as she glanced at Nick across a room she wondered if he felt the same. Once he had even come up and joined her when one of her old admirers was making a fool of himself.

'Look, old man,' he had begun suavely, 'why don't you shove off?'

Now that's wrong, Dana thought, except Nick's intervention had come as a most welcome relief. Come to think of it, *she* had invited Peter, but she had not expected him to assume he could hug her, or whisper compliments that were no doubt meant to be flattering but out of order.

'Dana!' a low, tense voice said behind her.

'Keith.' She had agonised over whether to invite him, but she never seemed to be able to keep angry for long. Besides, she had the unsettling ability to see two sides of a story, and it was obvious as she looked at him that Keith was suffering. 'I'm so glad you could come.'

'You look exquisite!' he said, staring down into her face.

'Oh, Keith!' she smiled.

'You *do*.'

'Shall I show you around?' She looked nervously around to see if she could sight Nick, but no doubt he had been carried off by some reckless lady. Probably the one who looked as though she had borrowed a dress from Shirley Bassey. 'I've invited April,' Dana said.

'I know that,' Keith answered stiffly. 'Please don't try matchmaking, Dana. I thought you had more sensitivity.'

'I know that she's a very attractive woman and really just the kind that you like.'

'Yes, possibly. But I don't think I could love her, Dana. As you so rightly observed, we can't love to order—or indeed common sense. I've always considered myself a civilised sort of person but right at this moment I could kill your McMasters!'

'*Keith*!' She put her hand on his arm, feeling the tension in his muscles.

'You have only to look at him! The insolence! Haven't you noticed the women are throwing themselves all over him, or don't you care?'

'I can't blame Nick for that, Keith,' she pointed out quietly. 'A woman would have to be blind not to admire him. I expect everyone is just having a bit of fun.'

'My God!' he turned slowly to stare down at her. 'Where's your pride? You can see what's happening here tonight. That woman with the dress that's sprayed on her. *Fun*, is it?' He clenched his fists. 'Do you intend to ignore a lifetime of infidelities? Of women chasing your disgustingly sexy husband?'

'Try not to let your jealousy get out of hand,' she said coldly.

'I've never seen such a flamboyant man in my life! And where's that woman of his, the redhead?' There was a vein beating in Keith's tight temple.

'I rather think she had the decency to stay away.'

'Really, Dana, you're peculiar!' Keith threw back his head and gave a harsh laugh.

'You haven't seen the library, have you?' Dana felt the glances on them with a terrible avidity. There was nothing more interesting than a developing situation.

Keith allowed himself to be steered towards the open double doors. 'Forgive me, Dana, I'm not myself.'

'*I* believe you're a civilised person, Keith,' she said soothingly, preferring to calm him down rather than have Nick do it for her. Hadn't Keith noticed that beyond the careless, insolent elegance Nick was built like a front runner?

'You've done a magnificent job!' Keith exclaimed, exhaling heated air like a dragon. 'How can you bear it? This was your home, yet you're forced to take a back seat while McMasters lords it over all the locals.'

'Please, Keith, do stop!' Dana begged, rather helplessly. She was, in fact, feeling very strained.

With a great effort Keith tried to gather the remnants of his self-control. 'Are you afraid to get out of this, Dana?' he asked.

For an instant she felt like screaming: '*Yes*!' but then Nick was in the doorway, standing still, watching them both. Then he was moving towards them with his particularly lithe tread, a sort of smooth glide that had the grace and impetus of a lunging big cat.

Despite herself Dana's fingers bit desperately into Keith's white-jacketed arm.

'Ah, there you are, darling.'

Dana pivoted towards him, her lovely skirt swirling out. 'Nick! I don't think you've met Keith yet, have you?'

Nick shook his head. 'I must now.'

Even Keith took a long swallow, putting out his hand as Dana continued the introductions. 'Magnificent party.'

'But you don't have a drink?' Nick turned and with one hand gestured to a circling waiter.

For a man who had professed his desire to kill Keith was looking considerably reduced. Almost a mild-mannered employee who could be hired or fired.

Unaccountably it made Dana mad. She looked up at Nick with suddenly flashing eyes and he, like a mind-reader, suddenly said: 'I *know*.'

Of course they had been capable of this in the past. A natural communication without words. They had used it as an extra sense.

Keith took a tentative sip and expressed his appreciation of the champagne and Nick answered him quite gently, almost as though he was aware of his inner turmoil and felt sorry for him.

'Oh, Keith! What *luck*!'

Nick got his hand under Dana's elbow just as April in a fabulous plunging creation wrestled her way through the crowd.

'You know April Radcliffe?' Nick asked him.

'Certainly.' Keith's ego was vaguely restored. 'I've been of great help to her.'

'She certainly looks grateful.'

'Terrible woman,' Nick murmured as he escorted Dana through the door. 'Gave poor old Radcliffe one helluva time.'

'From what I hear he got square. Cut her out of his will.'

'You're joking!' Nick looked down at her with malicious black eyes. 'No, darling, she got a great deal more than she deserved. Perhaps Vaughn can stick around to enjoy it. There's absolutely no sense in his grieving about you any more.'

She had moods for the rest of the night. In and out of laughter, despair. As though he had suddenly remembered her existence, Nick kept her clamped to his side, his public manner adoring, for everyone to see.

'I'm so happy for you, my dear,' Lady Kidston told her. 'Nick has told me so much about you—not in name, that was a secret, but a whole collection of piercingly revealing remarks. I only wonder he's stood it as long as he has.'

At midnight the party was in full swing and Dana gradually became aware that it was certain to go on until morning. The locals were great 'stayers' and Nick's particular friends, the Kidstons, Senator Reardon and his wife, the Mannings, the Campbells, the Bolans, the theatrical entrepreneur David Drury and his beautiful wife were house guests who could disappear whenever they wanted. Only the caterers were expected to stay on deck, for breakfast had to be provided for all who required it. A prospect that seemed even more enjoyable to many than the superlative supper.

'My God, I'm taking myself off,' Sir Bernard said at about two.

'A sober decision,' Nick smiled.

'Look at Clare now—in her element!'

Lady Kidston did appear to be having an immensely good time.

'Well, I'm off.' Sir Bernard clasped Nick's shoulder, then bent and kissed Dana's cheek. 'I'd like you to know I'm absolutely delighted about you two. Try as he did, Nick couldn't take us in. We knew there was a gel somewhere.'

'Lots of them, actually,' Dana murmured later. 'Do you mind awfully, Nick, if I abandon your party?'

'If you want to avoid a quarrel you'd better say *our* party.'

'Where's Jay?' she asked, her tongue loosened by champagne and tiredness. 'What happened to her?'

'I'm not in the habit of asking ex-girl-friends to my engagement parties.'

'Quite.' She began to laugh a little helplessly, putting one hand to her flushed cheeks. 'I daresay she's prepared to wait around until you're married.'

'*We're* married.' In full view of everyone Nick swept her off her feet. 'Shall I carry you upstairs?'

'Put me down, Nick!' was all she could say.

'Yes, dear, you go off,' Lady Kidston called firmly. 'Nick and the rest of us will hold on until the dawn.'

Inside Dana's old bedroom Nick lowered her to the floor and with one arm around her shut the door.

'Please don't do that, Nick.' She moved in to him gracefully so her hand could reach the doorknob.

'Oh, I think they'll allow us two minutes. Engaged couple, and all that.'

'It's not often one has a chance to be so happy,' she sighed.

'Come on now, darling, I can't come back later.'

He seemed too implacable to fight. His strength was frightening. He held her to him and she made no effort to resist. She even felt a violent pleasure that had to have something to do with perversity. 'So it's all settled? We're getting married?'

'Why, of course. People have been congratulating me all evening.'

'A marriage that could destroy us?'

'Don't let it upset you. One pays for one's sins.'

Dana flushed scarlet and the overwrought tears filled her blue-violet eyes. 'Let's see if you get any pleasure out of it.'

'You'll have a terrible time stopping me.' He pressed her head back sharply into the curve of his shoulder and kissed her with a hard dominance that made her crumple against him. He was taking almost completely the weight of her body, the severity of his grip hurting her, his mouth so demanding she began to move wildly.

'Damn you, damn you!' he muttered like a chant.

'*Love* me!' It came out in a frantic gasp.

'Oh, sweet God!' He bent her backwards and kissed the white swell of her breasts and she became aware now of the slight convulsive tremor in his body. 'If only. . . .' he said harshly.

Another minute and Dana thought she would go clear out of her mind, and it must have seemed that way to Nick, for he lifted her suddenly, walked halfway across the room, then flung her on the bed.

'Darling!' he said violently, his black eyes glittering against his abrupt pallor, 'the battle is over. And *I've* won!'

In the next month, Dana found her life was almost completely taken over. There were so many people who wished to please her by throwing parties, the days passed in a mad whirl. Even an engaged girl, ecstatic with happiness, would have had to be strong, but Dana in her unsettled frame of mind was becoming more and more exhausted.

'Damn it all, you're even thinner!' Nick told her when he came to collect her at the weekend.

'Perhaps my first flush of youth is gone,' she said ironically. 'Sure you don't want a young girl for a wife? I don't think I'm going to see the distance.'

He didn't seem to find it at all funny. In fact he, who had forgotten how to extend mercy, was shockingly kind. It unnerved her and made her travel back in time. If Nick turned into his old self she would die of grief for his lost love. The latest batch of photographs Keith had so religiously sent her showed that Nick was still taking excellent care of Jay Benson. Men were adept at leading double lives. It was a well-known fact.

This weekend they were house guests at the Kidstons' palatial beach house. The December sun was brilliantly hot and the Kidstons' house, built up on the cliff, fronted directly on to the glorious Pacific ocean and its terraced gardens led down to a secluded beach.

'Why, Dana dear, you're so fragile the breeze could positively blow you away!' Lady Kidston echoed Nick's sentiments. 'We shall have to look after you this weekend.'

And look after her they did. It was the first entirely peaceful time she had experienced in long months. She swam and ate and lazed, and Nick walked with her along the beach while the seagulls wheeled overhead and the balmy wind blew the sea spray into their faces. It was so perfect in its way, Dana was frightened to talk, and if Nick continued to watch her very carefully he too seemed loath to disturb their strange tranquillity.

On the Saturday evening all four of them went out to a restaurant for dinner, and Dana seemed to regain much of her old élan. Clare Kidston she had liked immediately, but Sir Bernard was not the tough and distant figure most people thought him. His attitude towards Nick was little short of paternal and to Dana he couldn't have been more warm or kindly.

Coming home in the car Dana even dared to take Nick's hand, and it had to be a dream, for he lifted it tenderly and carried it to his mouth.

'I don't like the thought of your going back to Richmond,' Lady Kidston said. 'I think, like Nick, and God knows my Bernie, you're a workaholic. It would give us the greatest pleasure, my dear, if you would look on us as family.'

That night she slept very deeply and awoke unexpectedly early feeling strangely at peace. The sun was only beginning its travel across the balcony and into her room, and the hypnotic chatter of the swarms of brilliant lorikeets was just rising above the dull roar of the surf. She wondered if Nick were awake, and as she remembered the odd tenderness of the night before, love filled her. If only they were granted just such another day, perhaps she could tell him how bitterly she regretted the wasted years. She could even tell him of her awful compulsion to protect her father. Surely Nick, who had loved his own mother so much, would understand that she *had* to protect her father even if he had deliberately set out to rule her life . . . part her for ever from her only love. After all, for four years she had survived in a sad world. The difficulty would be for Nick to accept that loyalty to her father was not the measure of her love for him. Quite simply she had cursed both of them in her bitter shock and grief. Now it remained whether Nick could forgive her.

Morning was shatteringly beautiful, yet the surf, so calm the day before, was white-capped and racing, the huge breakers a brilliant, jewel-like blue-green. She was an elegant, effortless swimmer up to a point but quite without an athlete's stamina. Still, she didn't intend to go far out. Unpatrolled beaches were wildly beautiful, but no one in their right mind took liberties with the mighty ocean or the sharks that headed in to the warm water.

White sand crunched beneath her bare toes and Dana slipped out of her enveloping black and white robe and stood for a moment in her body-hugging maillot, anticipating the exquisite moment when she would plunge in. For all the blue and golden heat of the days, the water could be surprisingly cold.

Waves lapped her ankles, licked her knees, then as a breaker began its high roll before her, she leapt forward into a smooth dive.

Glorious!

She surfaced, exhilarated, and pressed back her streaming hair. Could there be anything more perfect, more calming than these wondrous free gifts of Nature. For ten minutes she sported like a dolphin while the high-crested breakers rolled in more strongly. It was almost a king-tide.

As she turned to look back towards the house, a wave caught her and she went under, swallowing salt water, striking a knee and an elbow against the gritty sand. It was time to go in until the sea calmed. She didn't seem to be anywhere near as fit as she used to be. An excessive loss of weight, of course, had weakened her. It wasn't that she was eating less, rather an almost frantic nervous energy was burning the kilojoules up. She would have to make an attempt to slow down.

Another wave drowned her. The surf had become even wilder since she had ventured in. She was now swimming furiously, but incredibly making no headway. The sound of the surf was deafening and she prayed for a giant breaker to sweep her in to shore.

Oh, God, Nick she thought, where *are* you? She was simply swimming and getting nowhere, powerless to fight the sea. Please, Nick, help me. She was caught now in a rip and her courage almost failed her. Was it possible she was going to die like this? Drowning, helpless, never to tell Nick how much she loved him.

She *had* to tell him. She *had*! The ghost of an indomitable strength was returning. Come for me, Nick, she prayed. Come *now*. She couldn't bob helplessly for ever.

Another white-capped wave broke over her head and she thought she must be hallucinating, for Nick was beside her grasping her flailing body with hands of steel.

'Don't give up, Dana!' he shouted. 'Let go. I'm bringing you in!'

She believed him, instantly relaxing her body and he got his hand beneath her chin, striking out strongly in an angle across the rip. He was a powerful swimmer at any time, but the reality of death lent him phenomenal strength.

As soon as the ocean floor was firm beneath him, he picked her up and carried her in to the shore, the glowing bronze of his skin curiously drained. The seagulls still wheeled, the ocean was wild and glorious, and the sand glittered in the early morning light.

Nick carried her back to the shelter of the rocks where she lay gasping on her towel, every particle of her strength spent. She knew one thing for certain: Nick had saved her life. Not only that, to do it, he had put his own life on the line.

'Are you all right?' he asked quietly, when her breathing had eased.

My love, my love, don't leave me.

She was incapable of breathing the words, but Nick turned to her as though she had spoken, his gaunt face touched by a strange emotion.

'*Dana?*'

She moved her hand so she could touch his fingers, and only then did she begin to cry quietly.

'Darling!' He gave a groan and lay down beside her, staring at her with his black, brilliant eyes. 'Cry all you want.' He drew her full against him and she turned her face into his shoulder, pierced through with the tenderness of his expression. So long since she had seen it, she was unable to sustain it.

They lay like that for a long time with Dana drawing strength and comfort from his strong male body. The sun was full up now and brilliantly hot.

'You'll get burnt,' Nick told her gently. 'Let me take you up to the house.'

She opened her eyes and saw his beloved face. 'Thank you for my life.'

'I wouldn't need mine without you.'

They negotiated the upward flight of stone steps sown thickly with little golden-faced flowers, and at the top Dana leant against him and said: 'Please, don't let's tell Clare and Bernard—it would upset them. Spoil their weekend.'

'You look very white and shaken.'

'I'm all right.' She touched the curve of his mouth with her outstretched fingers. 'We won't tell them, Nick. A little make-up will work wonders.'

'All right, if that's what you wish. They *would* be upset. Why did you do it, Dana?'

She looked at him still dazedly, her lovely eyes as deep as amethysts. 'Do what?'

'You could see the surf was wild.'

'I've been in wild surf before.'

His bold face had regained its healthy colour, but his dark eyes were intense. 'It wasn't chance, coincidence that brought me down on the beach. You were calling to me.'

'Of course.'

As he watched her bemused face his eyes altered. 'We'll talk about this again. I think you should go back to bed.'

'I will lie down for a little while.'

'Fine.' He put a supporting arm round her. 'I'll

have to say something to Bernard and Clare. Nothing alarming, but a bit of an explanation. You got into difficulties—but of course I was on hand.'

Fortunately the Kidstons after their late evening slept in until after eight, and when Dana emerged from her bedroom an hour later, her hair bounced on her shoulders full and luxuriant, and a discreet application of blusher created an illusion of wellbeing. Truth to tell, she was suffering strangely little reaction to her moments of terror. She no longer felt there was some irredeemable grievance between her and Nick. She had clung to him on the beach, sobbing out her fright, their minds and bodies so close together they could have been a single being.

Desperately she tried to remember what he had said to her, but the words were as blurry as the haze she had moved in. It was his expression she remembered, the exact look in his eyes, and still that filled her with a rush of pure bliss. It reminded her of the days when life was sparkling, when her whole being brimmed over with the ecstasy of loving. At the end of a near-tragedy, she suddenly saw herself transformed.

Dana had no clear recollection of the rest of the day. They had brunch out on the spacious patio bordered by banks of flowering hibiscus and frangipanni; later they went down on to the beach with an ocean miraculously restored to serenity, and when it was time to stop talking and laughing, it was time to drive away.

'It's been lovely having you, Dana,' Lady Kidston told her. 'Any time you and Nick would like the house when you're married, it's yours. That's a solemn promise.'

Sir Bernard kissed her quite fondly and cautioned Nick to drive carefully. 'If only *I* could be young again!' he said.

'Aren't we going to the airport, Nick?' Dana asked him, when she managed to open her eyelids. The drive, so much sun and sea air, had made her incredibly drowsy.

'I think you've had enough for one day. We're going home.'

'Where?' She turned her head to stare at him.

'My place. Our place. God, darling, don't let's play any more games. You nearly lost your life today.'

'It was terrible for you,' she reminded him.

'The worst terror of my life.'

'I think I'll fall asleep again,' she said peacefully, in a little girl's voice.

'All right.' Nick smiled at her. 'The normal response to a trauma is sleepiness. Put your head back, darling. I'll wake you when we're there.'

Hours later Dana was standing on the small balcony of the penthouse marvelling at the night-time beauty of the magnificent cityscape. By day the vista was dominated by Sydney's incomparably blue harbour, but at night it was a fantasy of coloured lights.

'I hope you're ready for dinner?' Nick called to her. 'I've concocted my masterpiece, steak and salad. At least it's healthy.'

'I want the recipe for the dressing,' Dana said later.

'I refuse,' he smiled.

'You can't *possibly*!'

'I'll write it down.'

They took their coffee into the living room and Nick insisted she have a liqueur.

'I don't see why you want a wife,' she said with the dreamy sweetness so peculiar to the day. 'You've proved you're a very good cook, and you can take the laundry out, I suppose?'

'Isn't there something you're forgetting?'

'Apparently.' She fixed him with her glowing violet eyes.

'I love you,' he said.

She said nothing, but her eyes begged him to say it again.

'I thought there were only two things in this world I couldn't give up. You and the past.'

'And now?'

He was on his knees before her, grasping her around the waist. 'I don't want to hear anything about it. It's finished.'

'Because it was all my fault.' Dana leaned forward and kissed him passionately on the mouth.

'If you want to talk, don't do that again,' he said sternly.

'It's the truth, Nick.' She kept her two hands resting along the sides of his face. 'I let you suffer. I suffered. All because . . . all because. . . .'

'You wanted to preserve your respect for your father?'

'Yes.' Rather feverishly she kissed his forehead.

'He didn't have a serious heart condition?'

'*No.*'

'He took four years out of our lives.'

'Forgive him, Nick. Forgive *me*,' she pleaded.

He knelt silently for a moment, then he pulled her down on to the luxurious plushness of the carpeted floor.

'Nick. . . .' she whispered.

'I love you.' He turned her slender body right into his arms. 'Whatever I've done these last few months I've hated doing it. I told myself I had justification, that you deserved to do a little suffering when all the time I wanted you, as I've always wanted you, on any terms. Because I love you. Because you are *you*. When I saw pain on your face, the shape of your lovely mouth, I despised the man I'd become, the methods I used. All because you tried to keep your father's memory sacred. So little to ask of me, and I couldn't give it. I'm shocked that today was the only way to bring me to my senses. I don't know what I've become. I love you so much, yet I was forcing on you unconditional surrender.'

'Be kind to me, darling. Be kind to yourself.' Dana lifted her head and touched her mouth in ardent little kisses along the rasping satin of his jawline.

'Have you understood what I'm saying? I adore you.'

'Yes, Nick.' She pushed him gently and made him lie flat.

'*Dana*!' He groaned and put an arm around her.

'Do you want me to stop?' It was a very long time since she had made love to him.

'Never. But *hell*!'

'I love you terribly.'

Exultation flared in his face. One moment she was leaning over him, covering his face and his throat with tantalising, slow kisses, but even that ravishing sweetness was insufficient for his needs.

With devastating suddenness he reversed their positions, first and last the dominant male. 'Let me look at you.'

'Look away,' she said shakily, overwhelmed by emotion.

'You are positively the most beautiful girl in the world.'

'I don't know,' she said softly, 'there's Brooke Shields.'

'You can't be serious? Beside you, she's the plain one!'

Her mouth parted and she made a sound of longing, lifting her arms to wind them around his neck. 'Nothing can ever come between us again,' she whispered.

'Nothing else better try.' He put his mouth to her throat.

'Not even Jay Benson,' she said earnestly.

'Jay?' He drew back and stared down at her. 'Don't wreck this glorious idyll, okay?'

'But don't you mean to take care of her?'

'Hell, she must have a few thousand left. No, darling I don't think I'll be seeing Jay any more. She mightn't have shown her nicest side to you, but she had quite a lot of good points. She was totally devoid of deceit. The truth is she knew it was all over the minute she saw you. The most I could ever give Jay was affection and a good time.'

'And when did you last see her?'

'Last Tuesday, I think,' he said with complete imperturbability. 'It might be a good idea if you tell me what this is all about?'

'Nothing really,' she answered mildly. 'Someone saw you having lunch together.'

'They should have brought a tape recorder with them to check the conversation. Most of it was about you. I told you, Jay *knew*. She knew I loved you. Have always loved you. Will always love you. I think she was sad and happy both at the same time. Jay does have some feelings about me. I've helped her through a few rough patches. Actually it was a kind of celebration—bon voyage, that sort of thing. At the moment she should be on the high seas. Anyway part of the way to Europe. She enjoys boat trips and lots of attention.'

'I hope she finds a good husband,' said Dana.

'Uh-huh.' He gave a careless nod of his head. 'You're not really the most jealous woman in the world.'

'Don't you think you're just a little vain?'

It was exquisite agony drawing out the moment they would come together.

'Shall I give you Merrilands for a wedding present?' asked Nick.

'If you'd like to. I'd only give it right back.'

'Shall we sign it over to our son?' He began to slip the buttons on her silk shirt.

'Or daughter.'

'Which ever one follows their grandfather on to the land.'

'You have your sweetness back,' Dana said huskily, her body moving under his hands. 'Do that, darling.'

So beautiful. So perfect. Nick lowered his body and moulded it to hers.

A WORD ABOUT THE AUTHOR

A home perched atop a hill, a Jaguar, French champagne on the weekend, playing Rachmaninoff on the piano, scouting for antique furniture at auctions.... These are some of the elements that make up the zingy life-style of Margaret Way. She lives with her son, Lawrence, in Brisbane, Australia, where she works hard at her pleasures and takes great pleasure in her work.

She began writing to fill in the time when her son was a sleeping infant. She says, "I couldn't leave the house or play the piano, and I was too far away from my family to even speak to them reasonably cheaply on the phone. Always in my heart I had wanted to write, and what better way to occupy my time?"

There have been many, many books since the novel Margaret jotted down in longhand in a series of notebooks—the story that was to become *The Time of the Jacaranda* (Romance #1446)—but she has never looked back, regarding herself as singularly fortunate to be able to devote time to her writing. As she comments, "May romance continue to flourish all around the globe."